LAUREL-LEAF BOOKS

S0-BZW-451

Steffi and I are very close friends. She's the most important person to me outside of my family, and we never lie to each other, but this time I have to. It would be the end of the friendship if she even suspected I could possibly betray her. I know I wouldn't, but even just feeling strange about Robbie is so terrible. Actually, I don't even know what I feel about him, but something happened out there. Something outside my control. I mean, he knocked me out. That's it. My best friend's boyfriend knocked me out. Maybe that sounds stupid, but something happened between us. Well, maybe not between *us*. It didn't have to happen to him, too. Just me. Oh, I don't know. Maybe it was nothing. Maybe it was just something I ate. Whatever it was, Steffi has nothing to worry about. I plan not even to look at him. I'm staying as far away as humanly possible and then some.

FRANCINE PASCAL has written many books for young adults, including two previous books about Victoria Martin: *Hangin' Out with Cici* and *My First Love and Other Disasters*, an American Library Association Best Book for Young Adults. Both books are available in Dell Laurel-Leaf editions. She is also the author of *The Hand-Me-Down Kid,* available in a Dell Yearling edition. She lives in New York City.

ALSO AVAILABLE IN LAUREL-LEAF BOOKS:

LOVE and BETRAYAL & Hold the Mayo!

Francine PASCAL

LAUREL-LEAF BOOKS

LAUREL-LEAF BOOKS bring together under a single imprint outstanding works of fiction and nonfiction particularly suitable for young adult readers, both in and out of the classroom. Charles F. Reasoner, Professor Emeritus of Children's Literature and Reading, New York University, is consultant to this series.

Published by
Dell Publishing Co., Inc.
1 Dag Hammarskjold Plaza
New York, New York 10017

Laurel-Leaf Library ® TM 766734, Dell Publishing Co., Inc.

ISBN: 0-440-94735-9

RL: 4.8

Reprinted by arrangement with Viking Penguin Inc.

Printed in the United States of America

May 1986

10 9 8 7 6 5 4 3 2 1

WFH

For Laurie and Richard Wenk, with love.

I am grateful to my editor, Regina Hayes,
for her skillful insights and her friendly persuasions.

And a special thanks to Nina Colman
for actually suffering a summer as a camper-waitress
and being nice enough to tell me about it.

LOVE and BETRAYAL & Hold the Mayo!

This has to be the most exciting year of my life. For starters, I finally made it to sixteen. Mathematically, that should take only sixteen years, but with overprotective parents like mine, it seems more like thirty. Still, in the end they really came through. They gave me the most fantastic surprise Sweet Sixteen party.

My best friend Steffi helped them with the guest list, and what with friends and friends of friends and crashers, we had almost sixty people. My mother and father made all the food themselves, and it was fabulous. And the incredible thing was that I never saw them doing a thing. Even El Creepo (that's Nina, my thirteen-year-old sister) helped. Nobody seems to know exactly how she helped, but it didn't matter, because the very best thing she did was to go away for the whole weekend. Do you know what it's like *not* to have your thirteen-year-old sister at your Sweet Sixteen? It's the best present in the world.

The party was a sensational success. Everybody in school was talking about it for weeks. My father is a lawyer, and one of his clients is a music arranger for the Rolling Stones, and we had their brand-new record, autographed by the arranger himself. It hasn't even been released yet. It was the sensation of the party.

So was Jenny Groppo and her latest love, Robert Boyer. That's her fourth steady this year, and it was only May. She's probably going to have a thousand husbands before she's finished. Anyway, she and Robert sneaked off to one of the bedrooms to make out (guess which bedroom the dummy picks?), and of course you know who walks into his own room and turns on the light right in the middle of some heavy stuff. That was last month, and my father is still recovering.

Now the second fabulous thing is starting. I'm packing my trunk to go away for the whole summer. I'm going to be a camper-waitress in a summer camp in the mountains in upstate New York. Being a camper-waitress means that you wait on tables and get to be involved in all the camp activities. For all that, your parents have to pay only $740 out of the usual $1000 fee and the camp pays you a big $260. I know it's not a whole lot of money, but Steffi says the place is terrific. She knows because she's been going there for the last five years. It's called Mohaph. Sounds like an Indian tribe, but it's not—it's named for the owners, Mo, Harry, and Phil.

The job is a snap. All we have to do is set the tables and serve three meals a day. We don't wash the dishes or anything like that. Steffi and I figured it all out. You know how kids don't like to sit at the table too long, so they jam the food down real fast and then they're gone. We figured that each meal should take tops forty-five minutes from beginning to end, so that's forty-five times three, or two hours and fifteen minutes of work a day, and then freedom!!! After that, we can do whatever we want. Can you picture it—two hundred miles from home, completely on our own, with the easiest work in the world? And getting paid for it! I can hardly wait.

Another great thing is that I practically don't have to wait. I mean, we're leaving next week. The season doesn't actually start for another week, but we're going to get there early for a training period. Can't imagine what kind of training anyone needs to serve dinner to a few kids. I could do it with my eyes closed.

There is one small drawback. My parents thought the place sounded so great that they signed up El Creepo as a camper. It's a pretty big camp, though, so if I'm careful maybe I can keep far away. Except we're not even there yet, and she's giving me trouble already. I leave a week before she does, which means that anything I don't take with me she'll wear. I can't fit all my things into one trunk, but the idea of her dancing around in my best clothes sends me right up the wall. Of course, I can tell her not to touch my things, and, of course, she'll say she won't. In fact, she says she never does, but that's baloney. The minute I leave this house, she's into my closet. Not only does *she* wear my things, but then she has the gall to lend them to her gross friend Annette, a greasy-haired beauty who probably hasn't had a bath since Christmas. Just thinking about them almost makes me want to stay home. If only I could electrify my room. I wouldn't even mind barbed wire.

I had a thing with her just last week about my fabulous

new bathing suit. It's a one-piece, white with gold threads running through it, cut high on the thighs and off one shoulder. Very sexy. Anyway, I've worn it only a couple of times. I was saving it for camp. I folded it very carefully, and every time I looked at it, it seemed to be slightly different. I don't know, it just looked like someone was messing with it. Naturally I asked Nina, and naturally she swore she never touched it. The minute you ask her anything she always swears on everybody's life she's innocent. I try never to stand too close to her when she does that because, for sure, one day a bolt of lightning is going to get her. Anyway, I asked her nicely, and she denied it completely, but something about the way she said it made me suspect her.

"Look, jerk asshole"—I stopped being so nice—"I know you've been at my bathing suit. And if you touch it once more, I'll destroy you, Creepo!"

"I never touched your lousy bathing suit," she lied, "and if you don't leave me alone, I'm going to tell Mommy! And don't call me Creepo!"

"Try and stop me, Creepo." It makes me crazy when she straight-out lies like that. "Oh, sorry, honey," I said, not so accidentally knocking a pile of her newly folded underwear to the floor as I turned to make my exit.

"Maaa!" she shrieked, like she was being murdered.

And my mother and Norman, our giant sheepdog, came running. They almost collided at the door, and Norman went bounding into the fallen laundry, sending it flying in all directions.

"What's going on here?" my mother said, throwing up her hands and not waiting for an answer. "Can't you girls

6

get along for five minutes without fighting? For God's sake, Nina, how many times do I have to tell you not to throw your clothes on the floor?"

"She did it!" the little ghoul said, pointing to me.

"Prove it," I answered, staying very calm.

That did it. She went right into her crying act. She must have the most highly developed tear ducts in the world. She cries at least four times a day. She doesn't even have to have a reason—all she needs is an audience, preferably my parents, who are the biggest suckers in the world when it comes to their baby.

She did the entire number about how I always blame her for everything; I'm always picking on her, and on and on. Naturally I denied everything, because it wasn't true. She's the one who makes my life miserable with her borrowing and lying and snooping and everything. We had this big argument with my mother in the middle and, of course, she took Nina's side because she said you can't just run around accusing people without any proof, and on top of that said I owed the creep an apology. Of course, I didn't want to give her one, but my mother said I had to or I was grounded for the whole day.

There she was, the little creep, really winning, standing there in her room changing her clothes and telling me that I better apologize fast because she was in a hurry. And she had me, because my mother was standing right there, waiting. All the while she was unbuttoning her shirt and smiling that vomit smile, just waiting for me to start crawling.

I figured I'd make her pay for the next hundred years, but I was trapped right then, so I started to say how maybe

I had misjudged her, and she was lapping it all up and asking for more when she began pulling off her shirt.

"She's so mean to me, Mommy," she said, "and I never even touch anything of hers."

The biggest out-and-out lie of the century. And on and on she whined about how cruel I was to poor little innocent her. She pulled off her shirt and let her skirt drop, and my mother and I were standing there with our mouths hanging open. There she was, perfect little Saint Nina, standing there without a stitch on except the outline of my one-shoulder bathing suit suntanned onto her skin.

It turned out to be a glorious day. For me, anyway. Nina spent the rest of it in her room, contemplating the disadvantages of messing around with her big sister. She probably didn't learn anything except to cover her tracks better.

But that still doesn't help me with my problem now. I'm not going to think about it anymore. With luck, she'll get the flu for a week, and all she'll borrow will be my nightgowns. I decided to hide my best nightgown behind my chemistry books.

Even though I'm very excited about going, there are a couple of things that make it sort of hard to leave. One is Todd Walken and the other is Judy First. Todd has been my boyfriend for the last three months. He's terrific, and I like him very much. In fact, I more than like him, but I don't think I'm in love with him. At least not the way Steffi is in love with Robbie, the guy from camp. Actually, I don't think I've ever been in love that way. Steffi's just totally gone on Robbie. Not even interested in anyone else at all. She must write to him at least twice a day, and she doesn't even care if she never has another date with anyone else. I know I don't feel that way about Todd, but I am very attracted to him, and I certainly like him more than anyone else at the moment. But I know that the minute I get on that bus, Judy First is going to move right into my territory.

She's been dying to get near him all winter. She must have asked him to ten different things at her parents' club and anything else she could think of. But he always said no because I was around. As of next week, I won't be. Personally, I have nothing against Judy First. If Todd likes dumpy dodos with bananas for brains, dyed hair, and no personality, he's welcome to her. Wait till he tries to drag that klutz around the dance floor. Of course, there is *one* thing she seems to do very well, and often, and with anyone. If that's all he's interested in, he's going to have a wonderful summer.

Steffi says there's no point in working myself up since the only way to solve the problem is to stay home, and I'm certainly not going to do that.

Boy, I really hate that Judy First.

Why do they always stack up two good things and then make you choose? How nice it would be if everything were like this—would you like to spend the summer chatting with Nina or be a waitress in a summer camp? That's the kind of choice I'd like to have.

It's nearly impossible to decide what to take with me, particularly when everything I own is absolutely terrible. I must have the ugliest clothes in America. Even the things I pick out myself turn awful after a couple of weeks. Fortunately Steffi has some great things, and we're the same size. That's very important in a friendship, you know. And the best part is that she hates her clothing, too. So we switch. I probably should be packing her trunk and she mine.

Every few minutes my mother comes in to tell me not to forget my heavy sweaters and my down jacket. And my rain boots. I can't believe her. She must think I'm going to the North Pole or something. I shake my head yes, but I'm definitely not taking my rain boots. When will she ever learn that I'm not ten anymore? Never, I suppose. Funny, but sometimes when I hear my grandmother talking to my mother, it sounds like she's talking to a little girl. I suppose if someone is your child, they're always your child in some ways.

My Aunt Laura gave me a beautiful case just for makeup for my birthday. I figure my makeup will fill that plus a couple of shopping bags, and then I can buy things up there if I need them.

Besides leaving Todd and my family, I'm a little nervous about the camp. I know I have Steffi, but she's been going there for a long time, so she knows everybody and I know only her. What if I don't like it? I can't change my mind and just come home. I guess if it was awful I could, but when I take on something it's very important to my parents that I go through with it to the end. My father, especially, is very firm about not being a quitter.

I'm going to miss them very much. Even though you're sixteen, you can still get lonely for your parents. I know I did last year at Fire Island, especially when there was any trouble. I guess it's natural to worry about something new. And I'm good at worrying. I hope there aren't too many disgusting things, like bugs and wild animals. I've always lived in the city so the only animals I'm comfortable with are dogs and cats.

I am also going to miss Norman very much. Norman has been our family failure. Nina and I took him to a dog-training course when he was a puppy. He was beyond a doubt the sweetest dog in the class. He loved all the other dogs, even the most vicious ones. And he did get his diploma, but there was no question but that he was simply pushed through. You can say "heel" and commands like that until you're blue in the face and get no reaction, but there are certain words he understands perfectly—go out, eat, cookie, cake, bread, lamb chop, steak, ice cream, and get off the bed, Mommy's coming.

This is the first summer both Nina and I have been away at the same time. My parents are going to miss us terribly, especially when it comes to walking Norman.

"Who's going to walk Norman in the mornings?" I asked over dinner the other night.

"Daddy is," my mother shot back instantly. Then, in a sweeter, softer voice, she said to my father, "Well, darling, you have to get up at that time anyway."

"But not on the weekends," he said, and then matching her for sweetness said, "Mommy will walk him on the weekends."

"But I like to sleep late on the weekends, too," she said very reasonably.

By now, Nina had stopped eating her meatloaf, which

happens to be her favorite dinner, to pay more attention.

"Then maybe you want to walk him a couple of mornings during the week," my father suggested.

"I walk him every afternoon when you're not home." My mother's face was getting a little stiff. "Maybe you'd like to come home early a couple of times a week and walk him?"

I don't know if it was the meatloaf, or that he sensed the conversation was crucial to his future, but Norman pulled all one hundred twenty pounds of fur and dog up from his favorite nesting place under the table and stood alongside Nina, his chin resting on the table.

"You know, darling," my dad said, trying a smile, "I can't be stopped in the middle of a brief to come home and walk the dog." Feeling he'd scored a good point, he looked to Nina and me for a little agreement. Neither of us were dumb enough to take sides or to disturb the flow. This was too beautiful to end too quickly.

"Who's going to walk him at night?" Nina stoked the fire a little.

"Eat your salad," my father snapped at Nina, who hasn't eaten salad in thirteen years.

"Sure, Daddy," she said, actually spearing a tiny piece of lettuce with her fork. "Don't you think you should walk him at night if Mommy walks him every afternoon?" That would teach him to mess with Nina.

"But I walk him every morning," my father defended.

"But not on the weekends," my mother attacked.

"We could share the weekends," he offered.

"Oh, and what about the nights?"

"That's not fair," my father said, and that's when Nina and I cracked up.

"Good Lord," my mother said, "where have I heard that before?" And we all broke up.

That's the terrific thing about my parents. They have a sense of humor. They seem to have developed it fairly recently. Seems to me they took everything so seriously when I was younger. At least everything about their children. They're still heavily into the parent thing, but they're getting better at it. Better and worse. My father is still terrible when it comes to boys. I dread bringing home a date, because I can see that my dad doesn't like him before he comes in the door. It's like he's guarding the palace. Most of time I think he would like to throw all of the guys into a crocodile moat. A lot of them probably belong there.

Most guys I know are either creeps or semi-creeps. I guess there are a couple of okay ones around. Todd, for one. But even Todd can be a pain sometimes. Especially when we go out at night. We have a great time. He's a terrific dancer with a great sense of humor, smart, fun, and everything, and then suddenly at the end of the evening he turns into Dracula. Sometimes I feel like I ought to get myself one of those big wooden crosses to keep him away. It's not that I don't like fooling around, but unless you're really in love with someone, I can't see getting that involved. I don't know how I'd feel if I were in love, but so far it hasn't happened.

We have to be at the bus station by 7:45 a.m. For some reason, it's a group activity. That means not only my parents but El Creepo and Norman.

"Are you wearing jeans?" That's me, asking my mother.

"Don't start, please." That's my mother answering.

I have to explain a little about my mother. She's very pretty and very young-looking. Which is good. I mean it's ideal to have that kind of mother, but sometimes I'd like her to look a little more like everybody else's mother.

There's some last-minute craziness because Nina says it's my turn to walk Norman, but my father says it's obvious that I'm too busy, and Nina says something stupid like I'm always too busy, just to have the last word. My father is in no mood for her nonsense and tells her simply to walk Norman. She grumbles, whines, moans, and does the full Nina act, even throwing in a couple of quick tears. It's a tired act and nobody is impressed. Certainly not Norman, who simply waits at the door for the loser.

By 7:30 we're still not out of the house, and now it's getting frantic.

When we finally arrive, the bus station is jammed. It looks like a billion different camps are leaving this morning. It takes us forever to find our bus, and then I don't see Steffi. One bad thing about Steffi, and her mother, too, is that they're always late. Incredibly enough, they've never missed a train or a plane, but it's always a sweat at the end.

I look around but, naturally, I don't know anyone. My mother gets busy looking for the person in charge. She's always very big with people in charge. It's as though if she makes herself known, they'll know they'd better take good care of her child. Let them know someone cares. In this case, the man in charge is Uncle Roger, and I'm introduced to him like a six-year-old. Nobody really has anything much to say to Uncle Roger. The message has been delivered. This camper-waitress has a family, and a dog, and you'll be held accountable for anything that happens to her.

It's time to get on the bus. I'm starting to get in a small panic because Steffi still isn't here and I'm having trouble saving her a seat. Somehow, everyone seems to want that particular seat.

Big parting scene, hugs, kisses. Norman, in a frenzy, knows something unusual is happening and is pulling, not in any special direction, just pulling. That's a hundred and twenty pounds of pulling.

Steffi finally arrives. There's all kinds of squealing and hugging and kissing. Obviously, my friend Steffi is very popular. Strangely enough, this makes me a little uneasy. Not that I'm jealous, that's not it, it's just that she's the only one I know at camp, and I'm not anxious to share her with a million other people.

And that's what happens right away. I'm saving her a seat next to me, but though she dumps all her stuff on it, she whispers that she's going to sit with Ellen Rafferty for a bit. Ellen lives next door to the famous Robbie in Connecticut, and Steffi's dying for information. I can understand. I really can.

The bus pulls away, and my wonderful parents, fabulous sister, and brilliant dog get smaller and smaller and further away. Two minutes into the summer and I hate the whole thing, because my best friend is sitting next to someone else. Can you be sixteen and six at the same time? The only thing left is a few tears, which I could easily work up. I don't, though. Instead I bury my head in my new book, but that's all I can do because I have to keep my eyes closed. I get nauseous if I read in a car or a bus.

Funny how people look when you meet them for the first time. After you get to know them, they never look the same again. Right now I look around and everyone seems sort of formal and cold, like they could never be my friends. They all look much older, too. That's possible, because camper-waitresses can be as old as seventeen. I hope I'm not the youngest. I can see right away that one girl looks, at most, twelve. There's always someone who looks so young, and then you find out that they're really seventeen. Even when they're twenty-five, they still look like kids. I don't think I'd like that. Life's hard enough without having to explain all the time that you're really not twelve. This particular girl seems pretty nice and she's sitting right across from me, so I figure I'll act a little grownup and try being friendly.

"Hi, I'm Victoria Martin," I say.

And she smiles and says she's Annie Engle.

I go on with the usual things about how this is my first year up here, and how I'm sort of nervous about it.

"It's my first year, too," she says, and she is so natural and easygoing, I hit it off with her right away. She's got a nice innocence about her that's really adorable, and I know we're going to be good friends. With some people you can tell right away.

"Naturally, I'm a little nervous about the work because

I never waited on tables before, but the way my friend Steffi and I figure it, it's going to be a snap," I say. "Have you ever done this before?"

"You mean wait on tables?"

"Right."

"No, I think I'm too little."

"Hey, don't worry," I tell her. "I don't think it makes any difference if you're short.

Surprisingly, she gets really indignant. "I don't think I'm so short."

We're not even out of Manhattan, and I've had my first failure. I'm the Norman of the camp set. "I didn't mean it that way." I start falling all over, trying to ingratiate myself. "I always wanted to be petite. It's so cute." Once I start burying myself, there's no stopping me. "Tiny hands and feet."

Now she's really insulted. "I was next to tallest in my class last term."

I'm beginning to get a sinking feeling about my new friend. "What class was that?" I ask.

"Sixth grade."

No wonder she looks twelve.

I go right back to my book. Things are tough enough without latching on to a twelve-year-old. They must have put her in here just to trick me. Like a shill. God, I hate this place.

I'm sitting there with my eyes closed, turning the pages at the proper time, when I sense someone looking over me.

"That's a great way to read a book if you don't like it," the guy leaning over me says, in a friendly voice that has the little bumps of chuckles running through it. I like him before I can even twist around to see his face.

He pulls back and stands up straight. I was right, he is nice, tall and lanky, with silky straight brown hair that hangs over his forehead and always will. He's got a nice face. It's not gorgeous, but lively and smart, with a few freckles sprinkled across the top of his nose to give him a casual, easygoing look. He must be at least six-one. Probably a tall twelve-year-old.

"I'm Ken Irving. I work in the front office."

"Hi, I'm Victoria Martin and I'm going to be a waitress."

"You mind?" he says, sweeping Steffi's stuff to one side and sliding into her seat. "You're going to be a waitress, huh?"

"Is that bad?"

"No, it sounds great. I guess."

Suddenly I'm nervous. "What do you mean, you guess?"

"Hey, I didn't mean anything." I can see I've thrown him off balance, which I didn't mean to do. "This is my first year here so I'm just guessing at everything. Waiting on tables sounds terrific."

I smile to let him know everything's all right. "You think so?"

"Are you kidding, it's great. I guess." Now he's smiling back, and I have to smile, too.

Waiting tables, what could be so great about a job like that—except if it's your first adult job? Not like babysitting or mother's helper or some other kind of gofer kid job. Being a waitress is the real world, and so it *is* great. Naturally, I don't tell him all that. He'd think I was off my nut.

"What are you going to be doing in the office?" I ask him.

"I'm not even sure. So far, all they told me was that I'd be answering phones."

"Boy, that's a snap. How'd you get such an easy job?"

"The usual way."

"From an ad in the paper?"

"Are you kidding? That's the easy way. We had to get my mother's cousin Caroline's daughter to marry Mo of Mohaph's son. Then Caroline put in the fix, and, voilà, here I am. How'd you get your job?"

"Obvious," I tell him. "I'm Mo's son."

And we both laugh. I like Ken because he's one of those people you feel comfortable with instantly. It's as if we're old friends after five minutes. Only trouble might be if he tries to make it more than that. Right now, I don't feel like it. I can sense a little something else from him, but not from me, not yet, anyway. Good friends, that's all.

And we're gabbing away a mile a minute, having such a good time that I don't even see Steffi come over. Ken sees her first, and he gets a funny look on his face. Uh-oh, looks like I won't have to worry about Ken bothering me. I think he just got zonked. Too bad, but I know there's no chance for him against Robbie.

"This is my friend Steffi," I say. "This is Ken . . . uh . . ."

"Irving," he adds, not taking his eyes off Steffi.

"Hi," Steffi says, open and friendly as always. And not noticing a thing.

Now, straight off, I want to make it clear that I don't have any real interest in Ken Irving. None at all. Not even the slightest bit, though I like him as a friend. A lot. But no other way. However, it does make you feel a little frumpy, dumpy, gross, and highly rejectable when, after spending fifteen minutes dazzling someone, one look at your best friend and he forgets you ever lived. And she isn't even trying. This is not my day. In fact, what with Judy First probably making out with Todd the minute I got on the bus, this may not be my summer. But I'm not going to let it bother me. After all, it's only my whole life.

While Steffi chats with Ken, I sit there not allowing the destruction of my entire summer ruin a lovely bus trip. Just as I'm being overcome, Ken reluctantly tears himself away from Steffi and goes back to his seat. And Steffi turns to me.

"He's cute," she says. "Do you think he likes you or what?"

"Or what what?" I kid her. That's her new thing, everything ends in "or what?" Last year it was "you know." When she gets these things it can sometimes take months to get rid of. And they're very catching.

"Seriously, Torrie, I really think he likes you."

Even smart people can be so dense sometimes. "He *is* cute," I tell her, "but it isn't me he likes."

"Come on, all he did was say three words to me."

"Sometimes you don't even need that," I tell her.

"Oh, Victoria, you're so romantic. You read too much. It doesn't happen like that. Whammo, and you're in love."

"How did it happen with Robbie? Didn't you know the minute you saw him?"

"Not really. At first I thought, gee, he's cute. Then after a couple of minutes talking to him, I thought, gee, he's smart and nice and even better-looking than I thought. By the end of the first date I thought he was gorgeous and brilliant and the most exciting guy I'd ever met. And when he didn't call me the first thing the next morning, my stomach got so knotted up I couldn't even eat breakfast or talk or even think. It was either twenty-four hour virus or I was in love. Since I didn't have any fever, it had to be love."

"You see too many movies."

We both laugh, and then Steffi gets serious. "Wait till you meet him, Victoria, he's so terrific you're just going to love him. I never met anyone like Robbie before. He's not like any of the people we know at school. Most of them are just dumb kids—I mean, all they care about is making out. But Robbie's different. He's a real person. He cares. Not just about the people close to him, but everybody. Whole countries, the world. If something happens in Afghanistan, it really matters to him. And he's ready to pitch in and help or donate something or write a letter or whatever. He's the kind of person who could be President. I mean it, he's so special. I really am in love with him, Torrie."

I never heard Steffi talk that way about a boy before. Even her voice has a different sound to it. You can probably hear the love. I'm really happy for her and I tell her so. "I can't wait to meet Robbie. I like him already," I say, and

I mean it. Anyone who's that important to my best friend is going to be very important to me, too.

Steffi goes back to her daydreaming about Robbie, and I sit worrying about the summer, watching the countryside zip past. The sight of green meadows begins to relax my fears. I've lived in the city all my life, and I still get very excited when I get into the country; show me a brook and I go nuts, or those farmhouses that look like the ones I used to draw in fourth grade. And the sight of a herd of cows just hanging out in somebody's front yard still knocks me out. Steffi spends every summer up here, so she's not nearly as impressed as I am. I think she'd rather stick with her Robbie fantasies than listen to my babbling about the beauties of nature, so I just stay quiet and take it all in. It's hard for me to imagine what it would be like living in any of these small towns we're passing through. Sometimes I think it might be a nice life, sort of easy, in a place where everyone knows and cares about everyone else. Somewhere warm and friendly, and safe, with lots of county fairs and hayrides. Or maybe it's only like that in the movies. Come to think of it, it might not be so great having everyone know everything about you. You can get lost in a big city if you want. Still, I think I might like to try a small town for a while. Maybe after college. Just to find out what they do in between hayrides and county fairs.

I'm so busy planning the rest of my life that I almost don't notice that we've turned off the main road and are on a single-lane country road. Everybody is grabbing stuff off the racks and putting things together.

"Another five minutes," Steffi says, stuffing her jacket into her overnight case.

"I'm so excited," I tell her.

"Me, too. You're going to love it, Victoria. It's going to be our best summer. Nothing but fun from early morning to late, late, late, late as you want at night. Nobody's going to be standing over us. We're on our own."

"Super! I just hope I can handle the work, though. I've never waited on tables before."

"Are you kidding or what? It's a cinch. It's not like you're serving real people in a restaurant. These are just kids. You just shove the food in front of them and they eat it in two seconds and then you're finished. Free! Nothing to do for the rest of the day but lie around in the sun, swim, curl our hair, polish our nails, and dress for fabulous parties every night. The hardest thing you'll have to do is fight the boys off. They're going to just love you, Victoria. Wait'll you see." With that, the bus pulls up to a big iron gate and stops.

"Are we here?" I ask.

"Yup, this is picturesque Camp Mohaph on Mohaph Road. High on Mount Mohaph above beautiful Lake Mohaph. Remember from the brochure?"

"It's beautiful," I say, and it is. We drive through the high iron gates up a winding tree-lined gravel road, and at the very top of the hill stands the camp. It's divided into two circles of bunkhouses, one for the boys and one for the girls. Both are fantastic. It looks more like a hotel than a camp. I thought they said it was an old camp, but all the bunks look brand-new.

From the bus, if you look down behind us, you can see the lake. It's small but sparkling, with a tiny island right in the middle (Mohaph Island, I guess), crowded with weeping willows that drip their long branches into the water. Along the banks there are acres of green lawns carpeting the hills, and in the distance you can see the playing fields, playgrounds for the little kids, and a gigantic pool shining aqua in the sun. Steffi's right. I'm going to love it here.

The bus pulls into the parking lot, and we all grab our stuff and, loaded like pack horses, slowly make our way out of the bus. Uncle Roger leads the way. The closer we get, the better it looks. The bunks are glossy white, so freshly painted they look almost wet. Each bunk has different color shutters. On the girls' side, wonderful violets, soft mauves and pinks, with an occasional splash of burgundy. On the boys' side, the bunks are also sparkling white, but the shutters are in the more traditional browns, grays, deep blues, and reds. I love it all.

With Uncle Roger in the lead, we all start moving toward the bunks.

"I hope it's the one with the mauve shutters," I whisper to Steffi. "It's my favorite color."

"Actually, these are for the campers. Ours are further back." For some reason Steffi seems a little uncomfortable.

"Great," I tell her. "More privacy." And I mean it. I'd hate to be in the first row with all the little kids.

Uncle Roger turns around and holds up his hands for us to stop. "Waitresses can head over to the right," he says, pointing toward a big, beautiful building, almost like one of those old New England meeting halls.

"Fantastic," I tell Steffi, "it's the best one of all."

For some reason Steffi is hanging back a little. Almost like she's trying to keep away from me. Maybe she's worried that I'll be disappointed because it's not one of the little bunks. I try to reassure her. "Steffi, I love being in the big building away from everyone else, and we'll have the whole place to ourselves. Just waitresses. Fabulous."

"It's not that building." She sounds positively glum.

"Big, small, it's all the same to me."

She mumbles something I don't catch and heads around the back of what everyone is referring to as the Social Hall. That's where they hold all the dances and entertainment. Terrific, we'll be close by the fun place.

I accidentally drop my backpack and bend down to pick it up; when I get up again, I see Steffi picking up speed, and without a backward glance, she disappears around the back of the big hall. She's acting strange. I hope it isn't anything I've done.

I turn the corner of the building, but I don't see her. She's vanished—I must have come around the wrong side of the building, because there's nothing here but a couple of rundown old ramshackle buildings in the middle of what looks like a garbage dump.

The buildings themselves must be old storage shacks that they don't use anymore. Half the shutters are falling off on the one closest to us, the front steps are broken and what remains of a front porch just barely clings to the building. Could our bunk be in the wooded area behind these shacks? It must be. I hope it's far enough away from this mess. I pick up my backpack and start walking around the back of the shack.

"Victoria . . . Torrie . . . here." A tiny voice comes from inside the first shack. Then a head sticks out, Steffi's head, then I see the rest of her.

"What are you doing in there?" I ask.

She comes out of the shack gingerly moving her feet around, searching for a fairly safe spot on the porch, smiling the weirdest smile I've ever seen. Sort of what "I'm sorry" would look like if it was written in lips.

I open my mouth to say "What's up?" Then it hits me. Suddenly I know exactly what's up, and it's not good.

"Oh, no, Steffi, I can't believe it . . ."

"I'm sorry, Torrie, I swear it didn't look this bad last year. I remember it as sort of quaint and charming."

"Yeah, like the Black Hole of Calcutta."

"Do you hate me or what?"

"I'll tell you when I see the inside."

I make my first mistake. I bound up the stairs and right through the porch. And I mean through it. My foot sinks down up to my ankle and sticks there.

Steffi helps me pull it out. I don't say anything. With one slightly scratched leg, I make my way to the doorway. And just stare. There's only one thing I can think of to say. And I turn to Steffi to say it, but I don't. Her eyes are afloat in tears. Nothing running down her cheeks, but one word from me would start a cascade.

"I just wanted you to come so badly. And you never

26

asked me what it looked like. If you did I would have told you, I really would have."

"Let me look again," I say, and go back to the doorway. That was my second mistake. Looking again. It's even worse the second time. I'm mesmerized by its awfulness. Eight terrible iron cots, most of them bent out of shape, with legs that don't exactly touch the floor on all four corners and sagging hundred-year-old mattresses that look like someone bought them at the prison rummage sale. Each bed has a small cubby next to it. And I mean small. Three shelves on top and a tiny cabinet underneath. Perfect to hold everything for a short weekend. A single naked bulb (probably no more than 40 watts) hangs down in the middle of the room with a broken piece of chain dangling from it. No problem reaching it if you're over six-three.

You can't lie to your best friend. "It's the worst, ugliest rathole I've ever seen," I tell her.

"Sure, it needs some work, but if we all pitched in we could do it in no time."

"Certainly—by Christmas."

"Come on, Victoria. All it takes are some pretty curtains, maybe a cute bedspread, and some throw pillows. We could even get some pictures and posters. Maybe my mother could send me my Stones poster. We could hang it right over this rough spot," she says, indicating a gaping hole in the wall the size of a bowling ball.

But Steffi is only warming up. She's got a million ideas on how to turn this dump into Buckingham Palace, but I've stopped listening. Instead, I'm hunting for the showers. But I can't find them, mainly because they aren't there.

The only thing in the back is one crummy toilet with a cracked seat, guaranteed to pinch you every time you use it.

"It's positively primitive," I tell her.

"It's the country."

"What country? Where's the shower?"

"Just outside."

"How just?"

"A little way . . ."

"Stef . . . fi!"

"Three blocks away. But they're very tiny blocks, Victoria. I know it's not perfect, but . . ." There's no way to finish that sentence.

I look around once more. It's dark and ugly. And then I look at my best friend Steffi, and I feel dark and ugly because I'm giving her such a bad time. Okay, so it's not great, but we could fix it up, and besides, what with all the parties and great things to do, we're hardly ever going to be in the bunks anyway.

"My mother had some material left over from my curtains she could mail to me . . ." I say.

Suddenly, Steffi's whole face lights up, and she runs over to me and hugs me. I hug her back, and everything is terrific again.

Then we both start to giggle. "It's the pits, isn't it?" she says, beginning to crack up.

"You think it's that good?"

"Nothing a derrick wouldn't cure."

"Or a bomb."

"I think they tried that."

28

"Well," I say, looking around, "which bed do you think is the best?"

"The least horrendous or what?"

"Yeah."

"Well." Steffi starts walking around the room, inspecting all the cots. "This is a tough one, but I think it would be terrible to be under the hole."

"You mean the rough spot?"

"Yeah, the rough spot. Anyway, wise guy, I think that side near the bathroom is the worst. This side has the most light."

"Mainly because the shutter is broken and hanging off."

"When it falls off, you'll really have some nice sunlight. Anyway, it seems to me that far and away the best bed in the bunk is . . ."

And just as Steffi is announcing her choice and pointing to the bed in the far corner nearest the door, a very pretty blond girl sweeps in and, with one quick survey of the room, flings her stuff down on the very bed Steffi was pointing to.

"That one!" Steffi finishes too late.

"Are you referring to my bed?" the yellow-haired girl asks, in an accent that's a cross between phony American and phony British and sincerely mean.

"It's okay." Steffi smiles. "Hi, welcome to the Black Hole of Calcutta. I'm Steffi Klinger, and this is my friend Victoria Martin."

"I'm Dena Joyce Fuller," she announces, with such aplomb that I feel we should applaud.

There's a tiny silence. She seems to be waiting. Maybe she thinks we should applaud, too.

Before anything more can be said, another girl comes in, and while Steffi and I stand there, grabs the second-best bed, and within ten seconds, four more girls race in, and the next thing we know we're stuck with the only two beds left in the bunk. One is next to the toilet, and the other is under the hole in the wall.

We both shrug and move to the closest bed. There's no real choice, since they're both such beauties. I end up under the hole. I hope nothing big crawls in while I'm sleeping.

There's a lot of introductions around, and with the exception of Dena Joyce and maybe Claire, everyone else seems pretty okay.

There's a Liza from New Jersey who Steffi knows from last year. They were in the same bunk. And the Mackinow twins—I'll never learn to tell them apart. Alexandra from Boston, who looks very nice, and Claire, who's got a black mark against her from the beginning. She's a friend of Dena Joyce's, a Miss Perfect type. I can tell already we're not going to hit it off.

Before anyone can unpack, the PA starts screaming a frantic announcement. "Attention all camper-waitresses. Attention all camper-waitresses."

"My God!" I say. "What's wrong?"

"It's nothing, take it easy," Steffi says. "It's only Edna at the office. She always makes everything sound like a five-alarm fire."

"You should hear her when she's really excited," Liza says, and then she starts laughing about some time last year, but it's cut off by the rest of Edna's announcement.

"All camper-waitresses report to the flagpole. Immediately. Right this minute! On the double! Let's go, girls! Ten . . . nine . . . eight . . . seven . . . Move it, girls! . . . six . . ."

"Hurry, everybody!" Steffi shouts, flinging her bags on the cot, grabbing my hand and yanking me out the door. "It's the gargoyles."

"Oh, no," Liza moans, flying after us. Now everybody, even the cool Dena Joyce, is beating it down to the flagpole, wherever that is. Steffi's still got my hand, and I never saw her move so fast.

From all directions, the sixteen camper-waitresses come running. All the while the shrill commands of Edna can be heard over the pounding, panting girls. I'm dying to ask Steffi what's going on, but I'm running too hard to get out the words. There's such a mob behind us that we're almost rammed into the flagpole.

"What's going on?" I finally find enough breath.

"Later, Torrie, later. For now just stand next to me with your hands at your sides."

"Is this a joke, Steffi?"

"No, no. Not in the front line," she says, pulling me into the second tier behind two of the tallest girls in the group.

"I can't see," I protest.

"Neither can they."

Just then all sound stops. It gets so quiet you could hear a pin drop. That's even quieter than you think, since we're standing on grass. I can't see past the girl in front of me, but I see everyone else turn their heads toward the side nearest the administrative offices. I see them following something with their heads until the whole group is looking straight forward.

I peek around between the two giants in front of me. Oh God! I'm sorry I looked. I pull back and turn my shocked face toward Steffi.

"Nothing's perfect," she whispers, and snaps her head forward again.

So do I, only now for some reason the girl in front of me has switched places with her partner, and I have no trouble seeing what has to be the gargoyles.

Without hesitation, a broad-shouldered, two-hundred-pound monster lady, a hands-down winner for prison matron of the year, introduces herself.

"Welcome," she spits out at the quaking group. "I am Madame Katzoff, and this," pointing to a skinny little man next to her, dressed for riding in jodhpurs and boots and riding crop, "is Dr. Davis." The only thing Dr. Davis is missing is a monocle—otherwise he's a perfect old-movie Gestapo officer.

He smiles, and we're all ready to turn in our mothers.

"Who are these people?" I ask Steffi, but all she does is gulp.

Maybe they're just passing through.

"You!" Madame Katzoff shouts, and it looks like she's pointing in my direction. "You!" Again, but this time the shout has a built-in growl. Poor "you," whoever that is. I look around.

But everybody is looking at me.

I look at Steffi, and she shakes her head yes.

My God, I'm you. Someplace way back in the bottom of my throat I find enough of a squeak to answer, "Yes, ma'am."

"If you have any questions, ask me. That's what we're here for. Right, Dr. Davis?"

He does another one of those terrifying smiles, cracks his crop against the ground, and shakes his head. For some strange reason he doesn't click his heels.

"Now, your name?"

"Victoria Martin."

With that, Dr. Davis consults a chart he has, and stretching up on his toes, he whispers something to Madame Katzoff.

"Thirteen."

"Huh?"

"You," she snaps, "you're thirteen."

"No, ma'am, I'm sixteen."

"I know that, but your number here is thirteen. We don't use names. Now, thirteen. What is the question that was so important as to hold us up for a full . . ."

Dr. Davis supplies the time. "Four minutes."

In all my entire head there is not one question. So I just shake the whole stupid thing and say, "I'm sorry, ma'am, but I forgot."

"That will cost you a fifty-cent fine," she says, and goes right on.

Fifty cents! What is that all about?

"Let me read you a few of the rules and regulations that are going to make summer at Mohaph a joy for everyone," she continues. "Dr. Davis and I think the best way to start any day is singing. Don't you agree, girls?"

"Yes, absolutely," lots of heads nodding in agreement. It sounds okay to me. Maybe I misjudged them.

"Good," Madame Katzoff says, flashing a carnivorous smile. "Then be here lined up in front of the flagpole every morning . . ."

All right.

". . . at six-thirty. In your uniform, with the caps. Following the flag-raising and the camp song, there will be daily instruction and appointment of volunteers."

"Appointment of volunteers?" I whisper to Steffi, but I've lost her. She won't even look at me. Before I can poke her, Madame Katzoff launches into a list of our duties.

"Each waitress will have two tables . . ."

Not so bad.

". . . of twelve kids and three counselors."

That's thirty humans!

"She will be responsible for seeing the tables are wiped clean and set, the trays are washed, the glasses sparkling, and the Batricide room is spic and span . . ."

"Steffi, what's the Batricide room?"

"The kitchen after we disinfect it."

"There will be fifty-cent fines for the following infrac-/ tions of the rules," the matron, I mean, Madame Katzoff, continues, and for the first time both she and Dr. Davis smile. "Lateness, backtalk, peanut butter and jelly on the tables or chairs, spilling, dripping, unpressed uniforms, missed curfews, smoking, drinking, sloppy bunks, oversleeping, undersleeping, bikinis on the soccer field," and on and on she goes. I panic.

"I'll never remember all that," I whisper to Steffi.

Without moving her lips she says something that either sounds like, "Everything's going to be all right," or "We'll never make it through the night."

In pure Steffi style I ask myself, "Could this be a horrendous mistake or what?"

Okay. It's not exactly what I expected, but there are some good things about it. For one thing, I have my best friend with me for the whole summer. The rest of the camp is beautiful, I love the country air, Madame Katzoff isn't my mother, Dr. Davis isn't my doctor, and nothing larger than a mouse or a bat could possibly get through the hole in the wall over my bed. And I don't have to worry about them because, as I've been assured thousands of times, they're more afraid of me than I am of them.

These are some thoughts jumping around in my head while I try to unpack my things. It's not an easy job, because there is no possible way to jam everything into the tiny cubbies alongside our beds. Everyone has the same problem, so we all arrange to leave most of our clothes in suitcases at the foot of our beds, which leaves about an inch and a half of floor space in the bunk. There's sure to be a lot of knocked knees and stubbed toes this summer.

In a way, it's kind of cozy fitting everything into this little space. Luckily I brought up a couple of new posters and remembered to throw in some thumbtacks. First thing

I do is hang one of them over the hole above my bed. It may not be strong enough to stop the rodent invasions but at least I'll hear them, which will give me time to move my head so they don't drop down on my nose.

"You're not going to leave that vomitous thing up on the wall, are you?" That, of course, is Dena Joyce talking about my Stones poster.

"Not if everybody hates it. I thought it was pretty hot. What do you think, Steffi?"

"I like it. Liza?"

"Really hot. I have the same one at home."

Dena Joyce turns to her honcho, Claire. "Do you like it?"

"Yuk . . . it's the pits."

One for Dena Joyce.

Now she turns to the Mackinow twins. They shrug their shoulders sort of agreeing with her. They're funny, the twins—okay, but kind of like sheep who follow whoever gets to them first. Most twins like to be different, but not the Mackinows. They seem to do everything the same, even dress alike. Now Alexandra has the deciding vote. I'm not taking any chances. I get to her first.

"What do you think, Al?"

"It's okay with me."

That makes it even. I really do want to be nice, since we have to live together all summer, so I suggest we toss for it. Dena Joyce says heads and wins.

Later, Steffi tells me that Dena Joyce always wins. She's that kind of person. She's awful, but she always gets her way. You know how you see that happen in movies?

The bad person always seems to get her way.

I take the poster down, and now I have that huge hole again.

"That's better," Dena Joyce says, rubbing it in.

I'm stacking that up in the back of my mind for sometime in the future when I can pay her back. And I will, too.

That day, after dark, Steffi and I are alone on the porch. She's sitting on the railing, risking her life, and I'm balanced on the only step that's still in one piece.

"Are you sorry you came or what?" she wants to know.

"Absolutely not," I tell her, and I mean it. "It's going to be great once we get things under control."

"You're the best, Torrie. You really are. I guess I just didn't remember how, well, not perfect it was. All I remember is Robbie, and he *is* perfect."

"When is he coming?"

"In two days."

"Friday?"

"Yes, he's coming up a couple of days early because he knows I'm here. Oh, Torrie, I'm so nervous. I haven't seen him in six months. That's a lifetime. Anything could have happened. Maybe he won't be attracted to me anymore. Oh God, I shouldn't have cut these bangs. He probably hates bangs."

"Steffi, you're crazy. Those bangs are terrific. He's going to love them. I can tell from that letter you let me read that he wouldn't care if you had two heads and both of them had bangs."

"You think so?"

People get so different when they're in love. Normally Steffi is pretty sure of herself, but when it comes to Robbie, she's a mess. I guess when you love someone the way she loves Robbie, you always worry you're going to lose them. I've had crushes on boys, but I've never been in love like that. I worry so much normally that I'd probably be a basket case if I ever fell in love.

I don't know how she's going to survive the summer. He isn't even here yet, and she's falling apart. Well, at least I'm here to help her. That's what best friends are for, right?

"For starters, the bangs are great, you look even better than you did last summer. Don't you remember how that guy, Ken, on the bus went gaga for you?"

"Did you really think so or what?"

"Absolutely."

"He was sort of nice, but I hardly even look at boys the way I used to since Robbie. I practically look at them like brothers."

"I don't think he wanted to be your brother."

"No chance for anything else." She shakes her head. "Torrie?"

"Yeah."

"Can I dribble on about Robbie for a while?"

"No longer than a week."

"Forget that he's the best-looking guy you ever saw outside of a movie. He's sexy and he's fun, and best of all, he cares. He's the first one to jump up when anybody needs help. Torrie, he's like a hero in a movie. I can see him saving people's lives all the time."

"He sounds so great, I know I'm going to like him a whole lot."

"I want you to. You two are the most important people outside my family in the world. Sometimes I worry that you won't like him, and then I don't know what I'd do."

"Are you kidding? I like him already."

"Is he really as gorgeous as everyone says?" Dena Joyce says, carefully coming out on the perilous porch. Obviously, she's been listening. "Come on, Steffi, let's hear it. I'm really interested in Robbie Wagner. *Very.*" She sounds almost hungry when she says the last very. I personally will kill her if she goes after Robbie. I really will.

"John Travolta is almost as good-looking," Steffi says, without even a trace of worry. It's like a fat little lamb walking into a wolf's den. I wouldn't trust Dena Joyce with Frankenstein.

"He's just great . . ." my lamb friend goes on.

"Really?" says the wolf, practically salivating.

And Steffi launches into a description of Robbie that makes him sound like every girl's dream come true. Certainly, it's Dena Joyce's dream, and she's probably going to try to make it come true, but she hasn't got a chance. He really is in love with Steffi. I've seen some of his letters, and it's serious.

Still, Dena Joyce *is* very good-looking, the cheerleader type, long blond hair, blue eyes, good figure, just the way a sixteen-year-old girl is supposed to look but never does. Except Dena Joyce does.

Steffi's no slouch in the looks department either, but she looks more like a real person. Her hair is a rich dark brown, almost the same color as her eyes, and even without rouge she has rosy cheeks all the time. Her features are small, not perfect, but soft and nice. Sometime in the last three years she picked up five extra pounds and they stuck. I kind of think they're in the right places, but she's always fighting them. So far they're still there. Oh, well, it's a lot better than my problems.

I have long blond hair, my eyes are sort of greenish, I'm five-five and I weigh one hundred ten. Sounds pretty good, huh? It probably would be on someone else, but on me it just looks like me. It just doesn't come together like it does on Dena Joyce.

I would worry if Dena Joyce was interested in the boy I loved. But not Steffi. She rattles on about Robbie and doesn't seem to notice old D.J. drooling.

The conversation moves on to work, and Dena Joyce loses interest and goes inside.

After a while the lights go out in the bunk, and Steffi and I sit outside a while longer. It's only a quarter moon and very dark. The sounds of the country are nice. I wouldn't like to meet the noisemakers personally, but all together they sound good. I guess it's mostly crickets. I don't think snakes make any sound, or even mice or rats . . .

"What kind of animals are around here?" I ask Steffi.

"Not many. Sometimes you see a little garden snake or one of the ones that swim. And one time they caught a rattler near the pool. Last year we had a mouse in the bunk, and they say there are bats living in the rafters in the Rec Hall . . ."

"Bats?"

"Oh, don't worry, Torrie, they're just ordinary ones. Not the Dracula kind."

"Nice."

"And of course, raccoons and stuff like that. And spiders. Last summer we found the most gigantic . . ."

"I'm going to bed." And leaping across the broken boards and jumping inside the door, I hear Steffi in her most reassuring voice, "Gosh, Victoria, don't worry. They killed it."

"With what, a cannon?" I hate the country.

It takes me hours to fall asleep. There is just enough light for me to see the hole above my bed. It's not the most comfortable position for sleep with your head twisted up and sideways, but that's the only way I can keep a watch out for the invaders. There's not much of me they can get, since I'm wrapped in my blankets up to my eyeballs. It's a little warm, but well worth the discomfort.

Here I am, just where I begged to be. It's all my parents' fault. Don't they know how to hold on to a position? If they didn't want me to go, they should have made sure I stayed home. God, they are so weak-willed it's infuriating.

And on top of everything, that boy in the bus really dug Steffi. In other words, he didn't like me.

Last thing I remember hearing is the sound of someone sucking her thumb. Either it's a thumbsucking bat or somebody's got a very embarrassing secret. I'm sure it's not Dena Joyce; it must be Claire.

Of course, I have a nightmare. I'm camping out on the ground in the jungle in shorts with no blanket or flashlight. I wake up in a sweat. Before the full terror hits me, Edna, the lunatic lady from yesterday is screaming over the PA system.

"Let's go, girls. Up and at 'em! Up, up, up . . . everybody up!" And then the most horrendous bugle blast imaginable.

We all leap out of bed, racing in all directions, bumping into each other, rushing to get someplace, but nobody knows where.

Except Dena Joyce. She's the first in the bathroom, first at the sink, first at the toilet, and first in front of the mirror. Amazing!

The rest of us dummies begin throwing on our uniforms, backwards, upside down, and inside out. All the while Edna screeches on.

In less than ten minutes we're all dressed, most of us unwashed and uncombed, but ready. Heading out the door is the messiest group of waitresses, with the exception of D.J., perfect in her uniform, hair combed, teeth shining.

We make it on the double to the flagpole, assume our positions of yesterday, and wait for the gargoyles. I had forgotten how horrendous they were, but the sight of the two of them marching toward us reminded me.

We're sixteen half-dressed waitresses, shivering half from the chill morning air and half from plain old terror.

"I forgot to tell you not to put the pins in your hat," Steffi whispers to me.

"It's okay, I don't have any pins."

"Thank God."

"Tell me."

"We have to sing. Remember the camp song they told us about yesterday?"

"Why do you need a hat to sing?"

Suddenly she stiffens up and without answering me whips her head straight forward. Madame K and the good doctor have arrived.

"Okay, girls. The flag."

With that two girls, I guess old campers, walk to the flagpole. Carefully they take the folded flag and attach the two ends to the pulley. To the accompaniment of the bugle we all sing something about raising the flag once again at the break of the day. I still can't figure out what the hats have got to do with anything.

We hear a pep talk about how wonderful camp is, how lucky we are to be chosen, and what a wonderful summer we're all going to have. Coming from anyone but the gargoyles I might buy it, but I just don't trust . . .

"Let's hear it, girls!"

Steffi whispers, "Just watch me." Most of the girls are old campers and know what to do. They raise their right arms above their heads and drop their hands onto the tops of their hats. We, the new girls, follow and watch silently as (like they say in the books) they raise their voices in song. And their hats.

> Hats off to Katzoff and Da-vis,
> They lead a wonderful team,
> Rah! rah! rah! . . .

Three stanzas. I don't believe it!

Here we are, sixteen normal teenagers, singing and doffing our hats like idiots. Steffi is afraid to look at me. She should be.

Marching single file, still stepping to the inspiring beat of "Hats Off," we head toward the Mess Hall.

The Mess Hall is in a big white building at the far end of the campus, near the administration building. The eating part is one large room divided in half by a trellis-type wall covered with artificial philodendrons, thousands of shiny green leaves that look like someone oiled each and every one of them. Probably a perfect volunteer job for a camper-waitress.

The whole place sparkles with cleanliness. Each side has about fifteen or twenty tables, some round and some long rectangles. All are covered with shiny green plastic table-cloths, the same color as the leaves.

All the tables are numbered. Mine are seventeen and nineteen. They're in good places, not far from the kitchen. I just can't wait to get started.

We get to look at the kitchen, and it's empty and spot-less. No problems here. I can just picture how smoothly this is going to go. We'll just shoot through the whole thing, in and out in under an hour.

They let us do a little practicing with the trays. Even though they're a little heavier than I expected, still I feel very comfortable holding it. It's going to be terrific fun, I know it.

"That's super," Steffi says, when I show her my tray-holding method. "Someone show you that or what?"

"A friend of my mother's showed me. She was an actress when she first came to New York, and they do a lot of waitressing."

Now Alexandra and Liza come over, and they want a

demonstration, too. I show them the trick of balancing the tray on one shoulder so that it rests on the palm of your hand. They all try it, but it's harder than they expected. I've been practicing for weeks, so I've got it down pat.

I'm off to a very good start, I can tell. Sure, I'm a little nervous, but I know it's going to be great. I just can't wait.

Steffi was up at five this morning. It's Friday, the big day. Robbie is finally coming. The bus won't arrive until 11:00 a.m. but it's taken Steffi all morning to prepare herself. First she had to try on everything in her wardrobe. Naturally, she hated everything and finally ended up wearing a combination of my shorts, Liza's blouse, Alexandra's belt, and one of the twins (horrible to say but I still can't tell them apart—maybe it's really only one person breaking through the sight barrier) lent her a small suede vest. It looks great over the white blouse. The only thing I'm not crazy for are the shorts, but that's probably because they're mine.

Once she got the clothes under control, she moved on to her hair and makeup. She did at least fourteen different styles and ended up with the original one, long and softly curled at the ends, with one side pulled back. Except for the bangs, it's exactly the hair style she's been wearing for the past year. A quick hour to choose the nail polish and apply same. By 10:30 she was ready. At 10:45 she decided my shorts were wrong with the vest. At 10:55 she changed every stitch.

It is 11:00 now, and she completely loses her cool and changes back to the original outfit, half dressing, half running to the parking lot. Her vest is on inside out and the zipper stuck open on my shorts. Fortunately the bus is a few minutes late.

By the time the Greyhound pulls into the campgrounds, everything has been pulled into place. Now the zipper is closed—forever. Nothing matters except that Robbie is here. Well, almost. He still isn't off the bus.

I move back so that Steffi can have the field to herself. I step away, just beyond the parking lot, far enough to be out of the picture but close enough to be able to watch, like it was a movie. It's very romantic. I can't wait to see Robbie, to see them together. After all that messing around with the preparation, Steffi looks beautiful. A lot of it is her excitement and anticipation; it makes her face absolutely glow. It's hard for me to imagine someone making such a huge difference in your life. I've had lots of crushes but nothing that starts from so far down and comes out all over. It's great.

Steffi is all by herself out there, just like it *was* a movie and she's the star. The bus is more than half empty. I can see people inside getting up and reaching above the seats for their luggage. With the tinted windows it's hard to tell which one is Robbie. I'll just have to wait and see.

It rained earlier this morning, but now the sun is strong and there's enough breeze to spread the wonderful fresh country smells. It's not hot enough to make you sweat, and the breeze isn't strong enough to mess your hair; it's a perfect summer day. Perfect for meeting someone you love.

The first three people out of the bus are girls. The next

47

person is an older man and then . . . Robbie. It has to be. I can tell from Steffi.

Even though her back is to me, I know it from the way her body stiffens and gets alert. For an instant Robbie doesn't see her. He's expecting her to be on the other side where the rest of the people are. He searches them.

He's too far away for me to tell much. But I can see that he's probably terrific-looking, tall and slim, with a model's body—very sexy.

As soon as he spots Steffi he drops his bags and walks right to her. She's still nailed to the spot, but now she's tilted her head up to him. It's only a few steps away, so he's there in an instant, slipping his arms around her waist as she flows in and up against him. It's all one move. Steffi lifts her face to meet his and then her arms are around him, and from the angle of their heads I can tell they're kissing, and the kiss goes on and they move closer to each other, and I can practically feel their closeness. Now he takes her face in his hands and looks down at her, then kisses her cheeks and her forehead and then down again to her mouth. And stays there. Their bodies are pressed together, tenderly and lovingly.

Wow! I can hardly believe it's only my friend Steffi. It really is like a play. She seems so much like a woman, I feel I don't even know her. Maybe I won't with Robbie. Maybe she'll be so different with someone she loves, it'll be like she's outgrown me.

I'm so stuck in those dumb thoughts that for a minute I don't even hear her calling me. Finally my name breaks through, and I drag myself out of the fantasy I've been watching, throw on a smile, and head toward them, taking a new look at my old friend. She's beaming.

"Victoria," she says, putting out her free hand to me. I take it, and now we're on two sides of Steffi. Me holding her left hand and the great Robbie attached to the right one.

"My two closest friends," she says. "Robbie, this is the fabulous Victoria. And Torrie, this is some guy I picked up at the bus stop."

Now my smile is true, and I take my first close look at Robbie, the wonderful, the spectacular—

Oh . . .

Suddenly it's as if everything stopped dead and opened up, and I fell out. The air is humming and buzzing around me, or is it only inside my head? I catch his eyes, and it's like I touched an electric current and got locked into it. My God, Steffi! Surely she can see something's happening, but she doesn't seem to because someplace way back on the surface I hear her chattering on. I feel like I've been caught in a laser beam, something that stops me from moving or feeling anything . . .

"Victoria." It's Steffi's voice coming through.

"Hi," I jump in immediately, staring right past Robbie's ear.

He puts out his hand. "Good to meet you."

I don't dare look at him. I'll never be able to pull away. I don't know what's happening but I hate it. *Stop it Victoria!*

He's talking. Something about how he's heard so much about me, and on and on, and all the time I'm smiling a goofy smile that's directed somewhere between Steffi's face and Robbie's shoulder. Back and forth I go. Is he ever going to shut up?

Finally he does, and then they wait for me to take my turn. I say the same sort of thing about how much I heard about him. I take myself right up a blind alley, and then a weird silence falls and Steffi jumps in, and with a pull on Robbie's hand and with a kind of loving shove to me, gets us moving.

I keep falling behind, and Steffi keeps bringing me up alongside them.

"We got some beauties in our bunk. Something called a Dena Joyce. The pits, right, Torrie?"

That's easy. "Right," I say.

And for some reason, Robbie directs his next question at me. I miss the question because I'm bending down to tie my sneaker. Unfortunately I'm wearing slip-on sandals. They both stop to watch me dust my sandals.

"How do you like being a waitress?" he says to the top of my head.

I look up. They're both looking down at me, my best friend and the boy she adores, loves, worships, and will probably even marry one day. He repeats the question. I should look at him to answer it. But I know once I look at him, once I fall into that magnetic field again, I'll never get out. I've never felt such a strong pull to anyone ever. I don't even know what it is, it's so enormous. All I know is that it's not funny.

"Steffi loves it," I say. "Right, Stef?" That's the perfect answer. It turns it all back to Steffi, where it belongs.

"So far it's pretty simple, since nobody's here. I don't know what's going to happen tomorrow when the kids get here. I'm a little scared."

I'm still bending down messing around with my shoes, the same stupid smile still pasted on my face. Now I look up at Steffi, who is directing her conversation to Robbie, who is looking at me without a smile. It's probably only for a second, but it feels much too long. So long that I know I have to get out of here—and fast.

"Hey, I almost forgot. I have to fly. I volunteered for leaf waxing this morning." And, like I was a starter in a foot race, I shoot off, running at top speed.

"Leaf waxing? What's that?" I hear Robbie ask, but I'm out of earshot for Steffi's answer. I can't really remember if I made it up or they really have it. I'll volunteer anyway and see what happens.

I get back to the bunk out of breath but safe. I walk in to find D.J. alone, with her nose in Steffi's cubby. She doesn't even have the courtesy to jump when I catch her.

"Looking for something?" I say, like they do in the movies. At least that's what I mean to say, but I'm so crazed that it comes out "Looking for someone?"

"In a cubby. Really, Victoria, what's your problem?" And slowly, without one iota of embarrassment, she stands up, closes the cabinet door, and turns to me. "Did you get to meet the great Robbie?"

I can feel my face turning tomato-red. Dena Joyce has already turned the tables. There she was sneaking through Steffi's cubby, which is an absolutely disgusting thing to do, and instead of her being the guilty one, she's caught me doing something worse. In a second she knows something's up just from the color of my face.

"Not bad, huh?" she winks, and gives me a smile like we're both in on something.

"I barely saw him. He's okay, I guess—no accounting

for tastes, right? I mean, good-looking isn't everything. Or even being tall and well-built."

Please, someone stop me!

"Frankly, I go for an entirely different type. I'm not so crazy for that very dark hair, especially if it's very straight and shiny. I like curly blonds. And light eyes with dark hair doesn't turn me on. He probably lifts weights to get those kind of muscles, and you know what happens if you miss even one day, it all falls apart."

Anyone!

"Turns to mush right in front of your eyes. Naw, he's nothing much. Far as I can see, anyway. I mean, he's probably okay if you like that type. I suppose Steffi thinks he's cute. I mean, I know she does, but it beats me. Boy, is he ordinary. Just plain old nothing much."

Help!

"Absolutely nothing much. Even less. A minus, you know, a hole, a gap. It's like there's nobody there . . . you know . . ."

"Wow!"

"What do you mean, 'wow'?"

"I never saw anybody hit that hard that fast. Wow!"

"I don't know what you're talking about. I told you he's nothing special. He's . . ."

"Don't worry, Victoria, I'm your friend. You can trust me."

I'm lost. If D.J. is my friend and I have to trust her, it's all over. Then I remember that she really can't get inside my head. At least I can lie. I still have that left. So what if she doesn't believe me? Nobody ever believes her, and she gets by. "You can think what you like," I tell her. "It's all ridiculous, since I have a steady boyfriend for the last two years back home."

"Sure."

"Besides, let's talk about you. What were you doing in my friend's cubby anyway?" Now I've got her.

"Was that hers? Gee, I thought it was mine." She doesn't even make any attempt to give me a reasonable lie. And she seems to be enjoying it all. "Just like you with Robbie," she says.

Here she is, boldface lying, and I'm the one who's uncomfortable. We could all take lessons from Dena Joyce.

No point in continuing this, so I just turn around and get busy with my own things. It's almost time to change for lunch. In fact, if I hurry I can get out of here before Steffi comes back. I certainly don't want to see her with Dena Joyce around. I've got to pull myself together, or at least go someplace where it won't all show.

How is it that everyone can always read me so perfectly? Steffi's got to know there's something wrong. She has to. You just can't fool your best friend since the fourth grade. Especially if you have a face like mine. I need those Dena Joyce lessons.

"Torrie?"

Too late, Steffi's back.

"I'm so glad I caught you. We've got to talk."

Oh God. She knows.

"Privately," she says, motioning her head at Dena Joyce. "Come on, walk with me."

"Believe me," D.J. singsongs to Steffi, "the last thing I want to hear about is your marvelous Robbie. I've heard plenty from your very best friend, here. Haven't I?" That last bit directed to me.

"We better hurry, Steffi," I say, grabbing my friend's arm and pulling her toward the door. "We only have about fifteen minutes before lineup."

She follows me out the door, slightly confused. "She got a problem or what?" she asks. "What was that all about?"

"You better watch out for her. She wants everything that isn't hers." It really is the truth, but in this case it's not perfectly accurate. Still, it's pretty good thinking. In fact, it's Dena Joyce thinking. Now, if I can only handle what's coming now half as well.

Steffi and I are very close friends. She's the most important person to me outside of my family, and we never lie to each other, but this time I have to. It would be the end of the friendship if she even suspected I could possibly betray her. I know I wouldn't, but even just feeling strange about Robbie is so terrible. Actually, I don't even know what I feel about him, but something happened out there. Something outside my control. I mean, he knocked me out. That's it. My best friend's boyfriend knocked me out. Maybe that sounds stupid, but something happened between us. Well, maybe not between *us*. It didn't have to happen to him, too. Just me. Oh, I don't know. Maybe it was nothing. Maybe it was just something I ate. Whatever it was, Steffi has nothing to worry about. I plan not even to look at him. I'm staying as far away as humanly possible and then some.

"What's up with you, Torrie? You didn't hear a word I said. I'm asking you a very important question."

"No!" I answer, even though I haven't the faintest idea of what she asked me, but I'm not taking any chances. "Absolutely not. Not one bit. Never! No!"

"Huh?"

"I said no. N . . . O!" I practically bark it out.

"You don't think he's a little nice or what?" She's absolutely crushed.

Oh, I should have listened. "Oh, Steffi, of course I do."

"Then why do you keep shouting no when all I asked you was whether you thought Robbie was a nice guy?"

"Oh, I thought you were asking about Dr. Davis." There goes my Dena Joyce again. It's getting to be a habit.

"Dr. Davis? That monster! Are you nuts or something?"

"Sorry, Steffi. I guess I'm just starting to get nervous. You realize those kids are coming up tomorrow?"

"So?"

"Well, there are so many . . ."

"What about Robbie?"

"Right."

"Right what? Torrie, what's the matter with you? Do you like him or not or what?"

"I do."

"No, you don't."

"I swear I do. I think he's terrific, and gorgeous and nice and . . ."

"You hate him. I can tell. You can't lie to me, Victoria. I know you too well."

"Honest, Steffi . . ."

"He likes you."

"He doesn't . . ."

"Yes, he does. He even said so. In fact he was very interested in hearing all about you."

"No."

"What do you mean, no? Why shouldn't he? After all, you are my best friend. I want to know all about his friends."

"Well, that's nice. So, what do you think about . . . uh, Dr. Davis?"

"I'm seriously in love with him."

"Dr. Davis?"

"No, silly. Robbie. And I want to know what you think of him. I guess all that counts is that I love him. Still, I'm really curious about why you seemed so cold to him."

I can't believe she read my reaction as cold. If it was any hotter I'd have exploded. This situation is really out of hand—I mean, I just can't stand around talking about Robbie. Something's going to show. I don't know what's happening—all I know is that it's not good, but instead of feeling bad, all I feel is excitement. It was bad enough when I was with him, but now it's even worse just thinking about him. And all Steffi wants to know is why was I so cold to Robbie?

So I tell her the truth. "I don't feel cold toward Robbie. Not at all. In fact, I took to him the first time I saw him. He's exactly the way you described him." The truth is good up to a point: "And I know we're going to all be good friends." But no further.

"Really, Torrie? I hope so, because that's what I want."

I do her another D.J. and describe the wonderful summer we're all going to have together.

No way. I intend to avoid Robbie every chance I get.

57

When I think about him, I almost hate him. In fact, that's just what I have to do . . . hate him. I don't like Robbie Wagner. Not one bit! No way! No how!

"After lunch I said we'd all have a Coke together."

"Gee, Steffi, I'm sorry but I can't."

"How come?"

"I promised Alexandra I'd do her nails."

"That's okay, we'll do it after dinner tonight."

"Actually, I was planning on writing some letters . . ."

"I knew it! You don't like him."

"\ . . but they can wait. Hey, I'm looking forward to it. A great idea . . . a Coke. I'm thirsty already."

"Torrie, I don't know what's cooking with you, but something's weird, and since I'm supposed to be your best friend, why don't you try to tell me?"

"I miss Nick."

"Who?"

"I mean Todd. I really do, Steffi. Maybe I'm in love with him. What do you think?"

"If you were you'd know it, Torrie, you wouldn't have to ask. I don't have a minute's trouble about Robbie."

I really can't bear all these Robbie conversations. Everything turns into Robbie. "What if something happened? I mean, what if you just stopped loving him?"

"That's impossible."

"Suppose he stopped loving you? It could happen, couldn't it?"

"I guess it could, but I can't even think about it. It's too terrible. I don't know, but right now I think it would destroy my life."

"Come on, Steffi, you're only sixteen. This isn't the last guy you're going to be in love with."

"It might be, Torrie. Robbie is the kind of person I could end up spending my life with."

"You mean you would marry him?"

"If I had to decide right now, absolutely yes."

Suddenly I feel like I'm going to be sick if we go on with this conversation one more minute. Luckily, Edna on the PA system saves me.

"Let's go, waitresses! Lunch call! Hurry . . . hurry . . . hurry! Ten . . . nine . . . eight . . . seven . . . Move it, ladies, flagpole time!"

And the stampede begins again, this time with Steffi and me in the lead. Nobody is ever late for flagpole. Nobody. Ever!

Somehow I manage to get through the rest of the day without seeing Robbie and Steffi. Now all I have to face is tonight. I promised we'd all have a Coke after dinner. I'm beginning to work up to a major sickness. It's a tossup between lockjaw (which of course would be very handy for turning down a Coke) and some vague allergy that would make me itch all over. I start scratching right after lunch. Incredibly enough, nobody asks me what's the matter. It's almost dinnertime and I have red lines all over my legs and arms. Still nobody seems interested. Not even Steffi, who is so busy floating on air that she doesn't even know anybody exists.

"Don't forget about the Coke tonight, Torrie."

Unfortunately for me she hasn't quite forgotten everything.

I tell her I can't wait, and I hope that this terrible allergy (lockjaw is too hard to pull off, what with the clamped teeth and all that) lets up. She wants to know what I'm allergic to, and I resist the temptation to say Robbie Wagner. "I think it's something I ate for lunch or maybe some plant or something. Nobody ever knows with allergies."

"Maybe you should go to the nurse."

"I did already, and she said I should try to get to bed early and she gave me some stuff to put on." You see how one lie leads to another. It's like that Shakespeare thing about the tangled webs we weave when first we practice to deceive. It's too late with me. I'm finished practicing. I'm from the Dena Joyce school of professional liars, top of the class.

Tonight is the first night we're going to be formally meeting the boys, the junior counselors, the staff members—everybody except the counselors, they're not here yet. They ride up with the kids tomorrow.

Preparation starts for the big night at about four in the afternoon. Sometimes I think that's the best part of any party, getting ready. It all sounds so terrific when it's in the planning stage. It hardly ever works out that way. Even your clothes. You think you put together this fabulous outfit, a little something from everyone, and it looks terrific in your head, but somehow when it gets on your body it loses its magic. And then every little thing seems crucial, like even the color of your nail polish is going to matter. Probably nobody notices, but you can't take that chance. You need every advantage you can get, at least I do. But not tonight.

It's really tough to dress down, to try and look lousy. Lots of times I end up looking that way, but I don't know how to start off trying to look awful. It's harder than you think. I'm certainly not going to choose things that don't match or make me look fat or short. As a sacrifice, and to show myself that I'm really serious, I dress from head to toe in my own clothes. I hardly recognize myself. It's absolutely horrendous, but it is easy, and I'm the first one ready. By at least two hours.

"Hey, D.J. I love those velour shorts. They are hot!" Claire, Dena Joyce's best, closest, and probably only friend in the whole world, says. She holds up fabulous mauve shorts with pink satin trim. "Mind if I borrow them tonight?"

"Oh, honey, I'd love to but I can't. They're not really mine. They're my cousin's and I promised her . . ." It oozes out so sweet and drawly, Dena Joyce almost sounds Southern. And it's absolutely untrue. So far, every stitch anyone wants to borrow belongs to that famous cousin. She's just plain selfish, but Claire gobbles up everything D.J. says.

"Hey, no, D.J. I wouldn't want you to do anything like that. Gee, I know what it's like when you have to take care of somebody else's things . . ." And on and on Claire dribbles, practically apologizing for asking. It's really gross to watch.

"Honey," Dena Joyce says, reaching over and lifting the belt Claire has lying on her bed, obviously the one she was about to put on. "You don't mind, do you?"

"No sweat." She practically licks Dena Joyce. It's degalas. That's a French word that means disgusting, but sounds even worse, and it's perfect for Claire. "I like this jumpsuit better loose like this." And she sort of twirls around modeling what looks like a sack. "What do you think?" she asks the queen.

We're all watching, waiting for her to tell Claire, the balloon person, how marvelous she looks when she looks like a blimp.

D.J. takes a slow, long look at Claire. "No good, honey, you gotta put something around your middle. Otherwise," she says, snapping the perfect belt around her own waist, "you look like a glob."

"I don't think I have one," Claire says, like she really doesn't.

This is very hard to watch. If it was anyone other than jerky Claire I would jump in, but she deserves it for being such a nerd. I just can't believe someone could have so little character. It makes you want to throw up.

But Dena Joyce is perfect. All she does is shrug her shoulders, like too bad but it's not my problem, and turn away. Back to her curlers.

Eventually, one of the Mackinow twins comes up with a belt that works okay. I swear to you D.J. actually stops and checks it out, just to make sure she definitely has the best one.

"What do you think?" Steffi keeps asking me, every time she puts on something else.

"You look so fabulous tonight it doesn't matter what you're wearing. Did you do something different with your makeup?" I ask her. "A new blush?"

"No."

"It's something."

She smiles. And suddenly I know what it is. She's beaming. It's that love thing again. Too bad they don't have a counter of it at Bloomie's.

Finally we're all ready. Except for me, they all look great.

I suppose my mother would go bananas if she saw the bunk. Every bed has at least three rejection outfits on it. The floor is covered with shoes, curlers, hot curls, and blow dryers. Every flat surface is jammed with makeup bottles, jars, tubes, compacts: I would guess there was an easy thousand dollars' worth of eye shadow and face goo of every kind around, stuff to make your face peel, stuff to stop it from peeling, softening, hardening, opening pores, closing pores, special liquids that do everything except make you look older, which is what we all want. Steffi once used her mother's youth cream and worried for a whole day that it would make her look too young.

We head off in a troop to meet the enemy, the friendly enemy. Most of the time too friendly.

You can hear the music blasting before you're halfway there. It feels good—it's the first real sounds of home.

It's always horrendous walking into those things, even in a safe group like we are. I wonder if Dena Joyce has these regular human feelings. I can't picture her being nervous about meeting a boy.

"They're probably all jerks, what do you think?" Alexandra is walking with Steffi and me. She's a wreck, too, you can tell.

"I know one that isn't," Steffi says, winking at me.

"Nobody could accuse Robbie Wagner of being a jerk. Ever!" Alexandra agrees.

"And that other guy from the bus?" Steffi pokes me. "Remember him? He was cute."

"Except he was madly in love with you," I remind her.

Right away Alexandra wants to know who, what, and where. So Steffi tells her about Ken. She was really impressed with him. I thought he was okay, but not that good. She probably liked him because he was obviously so gaga about her.

I personally hate him.

"Sounds like everybody's there already," I say, trying to move the conversation off Ken.

"Get a load of D.J.," Steffi pokes me. And sure enough, there's good old Dena Joyce pulling out ahead. She's got to be first in everything.

"She thinks if she gets in there first she'll get the best one, like she did the first day with the beds," Steffi says, laughing.

"Right," I tell her, "but you better move it because the best bed this time happens to be none other than Robbie Wagner."

Steffi laughs and pretends she's making a run for it; Dena Joyce actually speeds up. Allie and I break up.

"What's so funny?" one of the twins wants to know.

Before we can answer, her echo joins her, ". . . so funny?" They're really strange those twins. It's like they're Siamese but they're not joined where you can see. They're stuck together at the mind, which is barely big enough for one anyway. It's the same person stamped out twice.

So I answer the closest one. "Nothing," I say, and continue to be hysterical. I still haven't forgiven them for the poster bit on the first day.

With Dena Joyce in the lead, Claire following respectfully a few steps behind, and then the rest of us, we go up the wooden steps of the Social Hall. The music is so loud inside they don't even hear us. Before they see us, we get a couple of seconds' free look at twenty-five boys, all brand-new. Excitement and terror.

Now someone spots us. You can see the word spreading through them. We keep heading in. They've become one large moving blur engulfing us.

"Smile, Torrie," Steffi whispers to me. Then I realize how tight my face is. It probably started off as a smile then froze into something horrendous. Something you practically have to chop off.

"Steffi! Over here, Steffi!"

I'd know that voice anywhere. It's coming from over my left shoulder, but I don't dare turn. Steffi starts to pull me toward the voice, but I say, "In a minute," and she heads off into the crowd. Now I'm alone. I make a quick search for Alexandra, but I can't find her. I'm on my own. Help!

"Hi," a nice voice says, and when I look up I see it's Ken from the bus.

"Oh, hi. How you doing?"

"Great . . ." He searches a second for my name, then, "Don't tell me. I remember. Steffi!"

Asshole.

"Steffi's friend," I say, as nicely as I can with one more try at being cute.

"Right," he smiles, "Steffi's friend." And he joins in the joke and he is nice. I get a quick sense that he's taking another look at me.

"Victoria," he says, and I think he likes what he sees.

"Right." I smile a real smile back and point to him and say, "Robbie!"

I can't believe my ears. Did I say that?

The instant it leaves my lips, the second the smile leaves his, I'm horrified. I really never meant to say that name. It jumped out of my head. I know his name is Ken, and I certainly know he isn't Robbie. Oh God, I'm getting crazy.

He recovers first. "Okay, now we're even." And he's back to smiling.

"Ken Irving," I say, to show him that I really do remember him. "How's the telephone business?"

"Great. I've disconnected twelve people in only three days. What's up with the waitressing? I haven't seen any of you girls in the Mess Hall so far."

"We don't start until tomorrow, when the kids come up. All we've been doing is learning the rules. You wouldn't believe how complicated it is. I'll never remember it all."

"So big deal. So you forget something. Don't be so nervous about it. After all, it's only your first time."

"Have you seen the gargoyles yet?"

"Unfortunately, yes."

"Would you like to make a mistake in front of them?"

"I don't think they'd do more than shoot you."

All the time we're talking, I'm watching Steffi and Robbie out of the corner of my eye. They've been dancing, a slow dance, real close. When the music ends they begin to make their way over to us. They're holding hands. I'm looking right at them, but I blur them out as they come closer.

"Hi," Steffi says, then I see her struggling for Ken's name.

"You remember Ken from the bus?" I say.

"Right, Ken Irving," she says, and Ken Irving beams. He's been remembered right down to his last name. This boy could never be interested in me. Then she starts to introduce Robbie, but it turns out they know each other already. In fact, they're sharing a bunk.

It's happening to me again. I'm . . . I don't know . . . upset by Robbie. When he's near me he seems to take over everything. It's really terrible, and I don't know how to deal with it. I know I've got to start by getting away from him; then I can think out a plan of action.

I barely wait for the new song to begin. "I love this song," I say, looking directly at Ken, who is hopelessly lost in something Steffi is saying. He doesn't even see me, but Steffi does, and before I can stop her she says to Robbie, "It's your favorite, too. Torrie, show him that new step you were trying yesterday."

And she pushes me onto the dance floor. Of course, he has to follow. But I stop it.

"I can't," I say to both of them (still not actually focusing on Robbie). "I twisted my ankle."

"I didn't know," Steffi says, concerned. "When?"

"Just before."

Steffi looks at me funny, like something's up, but I just go right on. "I gotta get something to drink. I'm dying of thirst. Anybody want anything?"

"I'll get it," Robbie says. "You should get off that foot."

"No," I say, taking full control of the situation. "It's better to walk it out."

"But not dance it out, huh?" Steffi's looking at me really strangely, but I pay no attention. I have to do it this way.

"Three Cokes?" I say, and head off without waiting for an answer.

I don't care what happens, I am *not* going to get involved with my best friend's boyfriend. No matter what, I swear I will absolutely not go near him. I swear on our friendship. All the way over to the other corner where they're giving out the drinks, I keep telling myself that this is the way it has to be. I have no choice. It's simple. I'm just going to walk away whenever he's around. I'll find reasons. They may not be fabulous, but it's better than what would happen if I stuck around. I know it. I can't control it any other way. I never had someone be so totally awesome in my life before.

"Torrie!"

Steffi comes up behind me, pulling me out of my daydream/nightmare.

"That's okay," I say, "I can carry them."

"What's up?" she says. "What's all this business about your ankle? There's nothing wrong with your ankle. You're not even limping. What's going on, Torrie?"

"Nothing. I really did hurt my foot, but it feels better now. I told you I had to walk it out."

"You're full of it. You just don't like him. That's what it's all about. I know it."

"You're wrong. I think he's terrific."

"You hate him. I can tell. You were practically rude to

him. I can't believe you'd be like that to someone who's so important to me."

"That's not true."

"It is, too, and you know it."

Here we are, the two best friends in the world, and we're fighting over something that isn't even real. I've got to stop it.

"It's because of Ken." I have to say something, anything.

"What do you mean? How can it be because of Ken? What's he got to do with your being so awful to Robbie?"

All the time she's asking that question, I'm thinking like mad for an answer. Then I find it. "I really didn't mean to be rude to Robbie," I tell her. "It's just that I think I've fallen in love with Ken, and he's all I can think of."

First I'm fighting, now I'm lying. It's really gross what's happening.

"I didn't want Ken to think I wanted to dance with Robbie because he'd just asked me to dance, and I got so nervous I had to say no, so . . ."

Just looking at Steffi's face tells me this is a dumb lie, but it's too late.

"So," I dig myself deeper into the hole, "I couldn't very well dance with Robbie, could I?"

Steffi looks at me; she's angry. I've known Steffi Klinger since the third grade. We used to have little fights, nothing serious, when we were really young, but we haven't had even a real disagreement since we got into seventh grade. I've seen her angry, but never at me. I just stand there because all the baloney is finished. This is really intense.

"I don't know why you're lying to me. And I don't know

why you don't like him, unless, and I think this is crazy, are you jealous of him or what?"

"Jealous of Robbie?"

"With me, I mean."

I don't believe it. I'm saved. She gave it to me herself. I know it's more lies but it's the only thing that's going to work. It's bad if I like him too much and bad if I don't like him enough. This is the only way out. So I take it.

"Well . . . I guess he *is* going to change our relationship."

"No he's not. Sure, maybe I'll be spending more time with Robbie, but we'll still have a lot of time together. After all, we'll be living together in the same bunk. We'll be spending more time together than we do at home, right?"

"I guess so, still . . ."

"Really, Torrie, and besides that, we'll all be together, the three of us."

Now it's getting bad again. I have to stop complaining. "You're right, Steffi, I guess I'm just not used to you having someone special, but really, when I think about it, I guess it's no different from the time I spend with Todd when we're in the city. Actually, you *should* be able to spend time alone with Robbie. I do with Todd, right?"

"Sure, a little, but most of the time we'll all be together."

Not if I can help it, but I don't say anything else. Enough. I'll worry about the togetherness later.

"Torrie, you're my best friend and you're very inportant to me, but gee, you can't do things like this. You know we have that pact that we tell each other when something's wrong. It would have been terrible if we lost our friendship over something like this. Something that could have been straightened out so easily."

I tell her she's right and how I feel so much better.

"Come on, Torrie, let's get back. They'll think something's wrong."

"Steffi, I know you're right about everything. And I feel so much better now, but I just don't feel like going back in there." And that's the truth, and Steffi sees it and tells me it's okay, she'll tell the boys my ankle was bothering me.

"You're my best friend, Torrie. I hope you'll be my best friend for always."

"I really love you, Steffi."

She smiles at me. "See you later," she says, and turns to go up the steps to the Rec Hall. "Take care of that ankle."

"Hey, gimme a break," I say, but she's already inside the screen door.

Okay, it's not perfect but I can work with it. The most important thing is to stay far away from Robbie Wagner and keep close to Steffi. It's a trick, but it has to be done.

I go back toward the bunks. The air is nighttime-sweet, filled with the scent of honeysuckle and grass. If only I didn't have this huge problem I really could be happy here. Tonight anyway. Tomorrow is another story.

Tomorrow, the kids arrive. They're supposed to come here about 11:00 a.m., in time for lunch. It will be the first meal we've ever served. We're all pretty nervous, especially since the gargoyles will be watching. Worse than that, they'll be eating there, too.

I'm so lost in my problems that I don't even notice that I walked almost all the way to my bunk with nothing but a flashlight, all by myself through the jungle. Well, compared to New York, four trees is a jungle.

I keep shining the flashlight directly in front of me and walking fast. If I weren't up to my eyebrows in all these other humongous things, I would have been scared to death to walk all by myself. It's wonderful how horrible things become okay next to horrendous things.

I'm the first one back and I hop right into bed so I can be asleep when the rest of them get there. I don't want to answer any questions. Especially from Dena Joyce.

The last thing I remember is pretending to be asleep.

5

We're all up by 6:30. Everybody's a nervous wreck, even the invincible Dena Joyce. And the day doesn't help. It's been raining all morning, not heavy, just a drizzle, but it's cold and gray and everything in the bunk feels and smells damp. All the talk has been about lunch—the first meal. Our big test. It looks like Claire is the most nervous, but inside my head I know I'm miles ahead of everyone else. Just the thought of remembering all those orders, balancing everything, and doing it all fast enough to serve lunch for thirty people (even if twenty-four of them are just kids) spins my brains and gives me a terrible whooshing feeling in my stomach. A little of it leaks out in a low moan.

Nobody can even eat breakfast and since then we've been just sitting around waiting for the big moment. The kids arrived early, about 10:30, and everything is different. The noise of all those kids settling in fills up all the empty sound space. I like the company. It brightens everything just to hear the excited activity.

"Ten minutes to blast off," Alexandra announces. Of course we've all been ready for hours. Then it comes.

"Attention all waitresses! Attention all waitresses! Report to the main dining room on the double. Let's go, girls, move it!" And on and on she goes in that hysterical World War III shriek. Boy, do we move it. Faster than that first day to the flagpole.

Again the stampeding herd barrels down to the Mess Hall, hands on hats, flying across the grass. I catch glimpses of kids coming out on their porches to watch the whir of waitresses.

From the distance I can see the gargoyles waiting in front of the Mess Hall. Madame Katzoff holds her hands up and we all screech to a stop.

"This is it, girls," she announces. "I hope you're ready. We're counting on you. Isn't that right, Dr. Davis?" And the little doctor smiles his assistant-to-the-killer smile, and everyone shivers.

"Yes, we're counting on you," Madame Katzoff continues, "and watching you. Now, let's hear it, girls. What are you here for?"

"To serve!" we all shout.

"And how are you going to serve?"

"Perfectly!" we answer as we've been trained.

"To the tables!" she shouts, and we all race into the dining room.

This is the first time all the tables have been set up. Going to be a lot of people, much more crowded than I expected. Jammed is more like it.

We already know which are our tables and head right for them. Even though I'm nervous, now I'm beginning to get excited.

I have the two youngest groups. One table of six- to seven-year-old girls and one of the same age boys. They have to be the most adorable.

I start setting up my tables. They're a little crowded, but the kids are small, it shouldn't be too bad.

I don't know why but it seems to be taking me longer than anyone else to set up. Maybe it's because Dr. Davis is watching me. He's making me so nervous that forks and knives keep sliding out of my hands.

"How you doing?" Steffi says, coming over to my tables.

"Are you finished already?" I ask her, and fall into a real panic.

She shakes her head. "I think my tables are smaller. I'll give you a hand." And she grabs some plates and starts helping me.

"How many do you have?" I ask, stooping down to pick up the same fork for the third time.

"About thirty."

"Me, too."

"You're just jumpy today. First day and all."

"Yeah." But it's her first day, too. I don't know why I'm such a mess.

Finally we finish. Actually it looks pretty good. In fact, I add a little touch for my kids by folding the napkins a special way so that they look like birds. Well, sort of.

"Trays, girls," Madame Katzoff commands, and we all rush over to the stack of heavy metal trays. Everyone takes one.

Somehow Steffi and I are last to get the trays, so we get the worst ones. Mine is crooked with a bubble right in the center that makes everything sort of slip to one side. Hers has a bend along the edge, the perfect place for a glass of milk to slide off. There is one tray in perfect condition. Claire gets it but it's just a matter of time before good old D.J. wheedles her out of it.

"Here, Claire, you take the lighter one," D.J. says, handing Claire an identical tray, only not as new and perfect and certainly not one ounce lighter. Dopey Claire says thank you.

Now we're all prepared, trays in hand, standing at our tables. It's very quiet and everything looks great. All we need are the kids.

I can't wait to meet mine. I love them already. I've pictured this day a hundred times. They'll march in, in double file, holding hands the way little kids do when they cross city streets on class trips; it's always so cute to see the tiny ones hanging on to each other. That's the way they'll come in, excited and happy. It's their first day and everything is going to be new for them so they may be shy and a little nervous, but I'm going to make them feel comfortable right away. I'll make some kind of announcement about how I'm Victoria, their waitress, and to ask me anything they need and I'll see that they get it. Anything, because they're my kids.

Then I'll take their orders. I've been practicing a kind of speedwriting so that I can take the orders fast. And I also have this method where I write down the seat numbers so that I don't have to ask who had what; I can just give it to the right person. And then I'm going to give them special personal treatment, like if one kid hates hot cereal,

I'll make it a point to remember and give him an egg or something else. I intend to be the best waitress in the whole camp. My kids are going to love me.

God, I can't wait. I know it's going to be terrific. It has to be, because what with this awful Robbie thing the rest of the summer is going to be very hard. At least I'll look forward to working.

Suddenly everyone gets alert. We can hear the kids in the distance. They're marching up to the Mess Hall, singing. Fantastic!

We all start to crowd up around the windows when Madame Katzoff announces stations.

We race back to our tables.

"Trays up!" she commands. Madame Katzoff never speaks, she commands.

We tray up and wait at attention.

They've stopped singing. We can hear them assembling outside the building and now they're marching up the steps. Sounds like a lot of them.

Suddenly the double doors swing open and a million campers explode into the dining hall. Involuntarily, we all pull back as they rush in, over, around, and through the tables and chairs. Alexandra is practically knocked over, Steffi is bumped into a chair, and I'm pinned against the wall. It's like a madhouse with the shouting and pushing and shoving, grabbing seats, changing them, rechanging them and all the while counselors trying to make some kind of order and then finally settling for saving themselves.

It's an invasion but it only lasts a few minutes. And then just as suddenly as it started it's over and everyone is seated.

I look at my little kids and I'm scared. They're all over the place. All my beautiful settings are scattered and the bird napkins look like they've been bombed.

It's hard to decide which table to start with: It's bedlam both ways, but I choose the girls' table because, I don't know, I guess I'm just more comfortable with my own kind.

"Hi, everybody, I'm Victoria, your waitress."

Nobody even looks up, they're all so busy shouting at one another. In fact, they don't even seem to hear me. I try again, this time a little louder.

"Hi, everybody. I'm your waitress, Victoria."

Still no response. Not even from the counselors. They're both too busy trying to make some order. It's madness with everybody jumping up and down again, changing seats, talking and shouting all the while. Two kids are crying, and one is under the table. This table is hopeless so I try the other one with the boys.

It's no better, maybe worse, except for one little boy sitting very quietly with the saddest face I've ever seen.

"Hi there, I'm your waitress, Victoria." I flash my big smile and shout.

The sad little boy looks up at me, confused. Of course, he can't hear what I'm saying.

One last try, this time at the top of my lungs.

"Hi, there," I give it all my power, and then suddenly, just like in that E. F. Hutton commercial, the whole place goes dead quiet, but it's too late for me. "I'm your waitress, Victoria," I shout into the silence.

And the entire dining room turns to look at Victoria,

the waitress. I stand there horrified for what feels like a month, and then somebody starts to laugh, and soon the whole place is roaring, and a second before embarrassment turns into tears, the real reason for the silence speaks up and everyone turns away from me.

"Welcome, campers," Madame Katzoff announces from the head table. Through my blurred vision I can see something that almost looks like a smile on Katzoff's face. For only a second, and then it's gone. She tells everyone how delighted she is that they're here and lots of other baloney, but nobody messes with her. They all stay at attention until she finishes and then it's right back to bedlam.

"Victoria!" the blond counselor for the girls' table calls to me.

I grab my tray and race over.

"Hi," she says, "I'm Carrie." She smiles and introduces me to Anna, the other counselor, who barely looks at me. Then she goes around the table telling me the names of all the kids. They're my kids and they look terrific.

Okay, so it started off badly—more like horrendous. So what? Now I'm going to show them what I can really do. I don't think anyone else prepared for this thing the way I did. I got it all down; all I need is to do it.

"Hey, everybody, we got a great soup today, clam chowder," I announce.

And they really respond—almost everyone at the table wants some. Fantastic. I feel like I just made a big sale. Eleven soups.

"Be right back," I say and rush right off to the kitchen. We have this arrangement where the waitresses line up in front of the windows to the kitchen and wait for one of the cooks to pass them their orders; but when it comes to the soups you get it yourself.

It works out perfectly because there's a line at the windows already, so I go right around and through the swinging doors into the kitchen.

It's wild in there. Everyone is running around grabbing plates and shoving them out to the waitresses. It's a little tough to find an opening to get through to where the soup pot is, but I wait a few seconds and then dart across. Sort of like crossing a superhighway. And almost as dangerous because the floor is really slippery from the spilled food.

I get to the soup and wait for someone to ladle it out for me.

But no one seems to even notice me.

"Jesus?" I say to the littlest cook. I think that's his name but he doesn't answer so I try "Iago," but still nothing.

"Can somebody give me the soup? I have eleven orders."

"Get it yourself, kid. That's what the ladle's for," the one who wouldn't answer me shouts, pointing to the gigantic soup ladle.

I don't understand how I'm going to be able to do this because there isn't even any place to rest the empty soup bowls or anything. But I got eleven people waiting so I have to figure out something. And then I remember that I completely forgot to take the orders from the other table. I don't know whether to go back and get them or get the soup.

I decide to bring out a few soups and then take the other orders. I'm hopelessly confused already.

I find an empty corner of one of the counters and put the bowls down and start to fill them. The soup is boiling hot, and by the time I get it over the floor to the counter where the bowls are stacked, I've spilled half.

"Hey, blondie, why don't you try holding the bowls near the pot," Jesus, or whoever, shouts in my ear, and of course, I jump and there goes the rest of the ladle.

"Oops, I'm sorry," I say, grabbing a napkin to clean it up, but Jesus has the mop and with one long sweep shoves the puddle of clam goop under a counter.

"Just get the soup and get out. You're in everybody's way."

"I'm hurrying, but it's just that . . ." but he's gone back to his mashed potatoes.

I load up the tray, but I can only fit three bowls on it because of the bubble. I've been practicing carrying a tray since I've been here, except I never had any real food on it. Especially not steaming soup.

The whole trick is to tuck your hand under the center of the tray and let the back of your hand rest on your shoulder. I think.

"Move it there, kid," Iago shouts, pushing past me. A spurt from every bowl leaps up and onto the tray. Forget it, I'll just carry it in two hands in front of me.

I make it back to my table and everyone is jumping all over the place.

"What took you so long?" Anna asks me.

I start to explain but she cuts me off. "Just give out the soups, will you? Everyone's starving."

"Come on, Anna, it's her first day." The other counselor,

Carrie, is very nice and even gets up to help me. Meanwhile the boys' table is shouting for me to take their orders. Please don't let them order the soup.

Carrie writes down the rest of the orders at the girls' table while I get the orders from the boys.'

"How's the soup?" Freddie, the JC, asks me. Everybody looks interested.

"How's the soup?" I ask-answer.

"Yeah," the other counselor says, "how's the soup?"

"Terrible, the worst, horrendous, and it doesn't even taste good," I say, and puff out my cheeks like you could throw up from the thought alone. Instantly everyone loses interest. It's the best move I've made all day. All day? All week. Ever since I got here things have been going downhill. Even on the bus it was starting to slip. This is the first positive step I've made. I would smile but I don't want them to think I'm kidding about the soup.

Carrie pokes me. "Hey, Victoria, I got the orders."

"Thanks, Carrie, I really appreciate it."

"That's okay. Here it is . . . two veal cutlets, plain no tomato sauce, mashed potatoes on one and fried on the other. Six regular veal cutlets, two with fried potatoes, three with mashed potatoes, and one with no potatoes. Four chef salads, two with Russian, one oil and vinegar, and one French . . ."

"Hey, Victoria." It's Anna from the other table. "What happened to the rest of our soups?"

"Sorry, I was just taking these orders."

"Victoria!" That's from the boy's table. It's the JC again. "How about taking our orders? We're starving."

"In a second."

"They're already on their soup and you haven't even taken our orders. What's up?" Now the senior counselor joins in. They all start shouting at the same time, and my brilliant plan of speedwriting goes down the drain.

I start to scribble things down, but they go too fast. Everyone seems to be eating the veal, but nobody wants it the way it comes, and then they all want something different with it.

"Don't we get any rolls or something?" someone else shouts out.

"What about some water?"

"And butter!"

"Coming—coming," I say and rush off. I would really love to run right out the door and never come back. I can't do this. I just can't. I look around and everyone else seems to be handling things okay. What's wrong with me?

Just when I'm rushing toward the kitchen I spot Robbie coming in my direction. That's just what I need. But he's heading someplace else. He gives me a smile that sinks my stomach, and passes.

I get on the back of the line for the food; then I remember I still owe them seven soups.

"Should I get the rest of the soups or stay here and get the food?" I guess it's dumb to ask Alexandra that, but I don't know what to do.

She says, "Huh?"

"I'm making a mess of everything. I just can't do it."

"Sure you can. It's really hard the first day, but you'll

see. It'll get better. You'll get the hang of it."

"What should I do about the soups?"

"Go get them. I'll hold your place."

"Thanks, Al, I'll do it as fast as I can."

I run back into the kitchen and start ladling out the other soups. I find a way of piling them to get six on the tray at once. In fact, I'm sort of pleased with myself. Maybe it's not hopeless.

Very carefully, I carry the tray into the dining room and over to the table. I stop behind Anna and start to hand out the soups. Just as I'm serving, Madame Katzoff rises and the whole camp leaps to its feet. Including Anna, whose shoulder sends my tray sailing up, out of my hands. Soup bowls spin off in all directions.

"Watch it, you jerk!" Anna shouts, but it's too late. The next instant she's coated with white clam goo. I grab a napkin and start wiping her off, but she fights me and only makes it worse. Little minced clams cling to her eyelashes, potato chunks dot her brown curls, and lots of just plain soup drenches her T-shirt and shorts. She looks terrible. And she looks like she's going to kill me. I edge away from her, but some of the clam slime gets caught under my shoe and I start to slip. I grab the nearest thing to steady myself. It happens to be Anna.

Together we swing sideways, way out to the end of the table like we're dancing, and then there's a scramble of legs and arms flying and we're on the floor. It's so embarrassing I don't even feel the bang of my bottom hitting the floor. But Anna feels hers.

"You dumb ass! Are you trying to kill me or something? You are the worst, clumsiest waitress in the world! You should be fired!"

"I'm really sorry," I say, trying to help her up, but she shoves me away and, grabbing a chair, starts to lift herself up. It doesn't work, and the chair turns over and she goes back down into the clams, even angrier.

Meanwhile I move back into the crowd of kids. No way to get lost in a mob of three-footers. We're causing such a commotion that counselors from the other tables come over and soon everybody's walking in clam goo and then a couple of the littler kids start to write in it with the backs of their forks.

Almost instantly, the kitchen cleanup squad come out with their mops. Anna, in a rage, storms out of the dining hall.

In no time they put the place back in order and everyone is starting to shout orders to me again. I hope they're going to wait to the end of the day to fire me. I mean, they've got to fire me. I'm the worst waitress in the whole country. I can't understand why I'm such a terrible failure. Even Claire is doing okay. At least she isn't swimming in clam chowder.

There's no time for too much inner misery because the outside stuff is even worse. At least I'm off the hook for the soup.

Nobody wants soup—ever! Well, at least not from me.

I finish taking the orders and hurry back to the line. It's even longer now. My table, my people, my kids, the ones I really wanted to love and to give the best special service and everything, are doomed—under my special care they'll probably starve to death.

"Hey, it's the clam kid," Jesus shouts when he sees me, and the rest of the kitchen turns around and it's all the big joke. Only trouble is, it's me that's so funny.

"May I please have . . ."

"Let's hear it, baby. Fast, speed it up, kid. There's hungry people out there and I got a hot date this afternoon."

I start to read off the orders, and then I get to the ones Carrie wrote down, and I can't read a word. It's all chicken scratch.

"Come on, baby. I haven't got all day."

But I can't read it. "Could you just start on those and I'll be right back?" I shoot to the table without waiting for an answer.

My heart drops when I pass Steffi's table. I'm lost. They're eating dessert!

By the time I get back to the kitchen window, Jesus is shoving plates of veal out at me. I grab as many as I can, piling them on the tray so that I get eight on at once. That's pretty good stacking.

Feeling a little better, I spin around and head forward. As I do, one full plate of veal flies off my tray and lands neatly in the giant garbage pail. I give a quick look around. Nobody saw. That's it, gone—plate and all. I keep moving. Seven's not so bad either.

"Who had the veal without the sauce?" I ask the boys' table.

Nobody can remember. Well, they're only seven years old. What can you expect? They're just little kids.

"How about the veal with the sauce?"

They all raise their hands and start shouting, "Me . . . me! Me!"

I know I got some orders for the veal without sauce, but what can I do? Even Carrie is beginning to look at me funny. I've been doing everything else wrong, why not this, too? I grab the three sauceless veals and race back, shove them at Jesus for saucing, grab what he has, pile them on the tray, shoot back to the tables, give them out, and get right back to pick up the rest of the orders. I'm up to my eyebrows in tomato sauce, clam stuff all over my shorts, a band of assorted mess across my middle where I lean the tray, and four french fries in my pocket.

My tables are just getting their main courses and everyone is finishing dessert. I don't know how everyone else is doing it because I can't take even a second to look. I haven't seen Steffi since this all started. She must be so disappointed in me. She recommended a horror.

"How many desserts?" I ask, even though they've just started their veal.

"We're not going to have time for desserts, kids. We have to get to the Rec Hall before one-thirty," Carrie explains to the table. Did you ever try to tell seven-year-olds that they can't have chocolate pudding? There's plenty of grumbling and complaining. It's all my fault, so naturally they hate me. I'm so exhausted I'd rather have them hate me than get twenty-four desserts.

There's a lot of furious eating, more bread, more milk, more butter, another knife, and on and on. I keep running back and forth. Finally, they finish. Just like that, and instantly they're gone. Mine are the last tables to leave. Steffi has already cleaned up hers.

"Victoria."

I can tell from the way she calls my name that she knows how bad it's been. One look at her face and I know it's been even worse than I thought.

"Don't worry," she says, shaking her head and smiling. "It's going to get better. Everybody starts off the same."

"That's not true, Steffi, nobody made a mess like I did. Even Claire was better than I was."

Poor Steffi, she doesn't know what to say. It's all true. I'm hopeless. She makes some noises about how I'll look back at all this and laugh, but I probably won't get the chance since they'll certainly fire me today anyway.

"Torrie, do you want me to help you or what?"

"Aren't you supposed to meet Robbie now?"

"Yeah, but that's okay. He'll understand."

"Thanks, but I think it's important that I handle it by myself. I'll catch you later back at the bunk."

I don't have to convince her, because she's so anxious to spend time with Robbie. Boy, can I understand that. All too well.

All you have to do is take one look at my tables and you know why nobody is fighting to get the little kids' group. It's a garbage heap. They do more eating on the table than on their plates.

I dive into the job and after what seems like fifty trips to the kitchen I finally get the tables emptied and ready for dinner setup. No more fancy bird napkins, I'm just happy to get the necessary things on the table. What difference does it make since they hate me already? And I'm not so crazy about them, either. Except for one little boy. His name was Henry, and he looked the way I feel inside now. Very sad. I hate being a failure. I wonder what his problem is?

I drag myself back to the bunk and everyone else is sunbathing outside, giggling and talking. I'm exhausted.

"Victoria Martin?" Liana, one of the women who works in the office pokes her head in the bunk.

"That's me."

"I think you have volunteer mail delivery."

"Volunteer? I don't think I volunteered for anything yet."

"Nobody really does," she says very apologetically. "They just sort of assign the volunteers, but you don't have to if you don't want to. It's not part of your job. You can explain to Madame Katzoff if you . . ."

"Explain to Madame Katzoff? Oh, no! I love mail delivery. I really do." I jump off the bed. "I'm ready right now."

"Great. You can pick up the sacks at the front office." And she's gone.

I sink back on my bed. Sixteen-year-olds don't cry, I tell myself, but it doesn't really help much. I know I wouldn't feel so awful if I'd done a better job. And now I have to worry about screwing up mail delivery. Sounds easy, but in my hands it'll probably be a disaster.

I change into my jeans and head over to the office. There are three other "volunteers" there, but they've already gotten their sacks and started by the time I arrive. The only sack left is the unbunked one. Unbunked means that it's just the camper's name. You have to look up the bunk numbers on the master sheet and then give them out.

This job takes me from 2:30 until after 4:00, which gives me about a half hour to get washed up and ready for dinner setup.

"Victoria." That's Alexandra. She's in her bathing suit. "I was just going down for a swim. How about it? I'll wait if you want."

Besides the fact that I'd probably sink right down to the bottom from exhaustion, I can't go swimming, ever—Robbie's there. He's in charge of the waterfront. So that's it. Summer camp without the water. Great, huh?

"Thanks, Al, but I'm beat."

"Sure thing, see you later." And she's off.

The bunk is empty and the quiet feels good. I refuse to allow my mind to go over the horrendous things that have happened so far and I'm not thinking about dinner because that's too terrifying. Of course, I'm not thinking about the Robbie problem or the fact that it's just a matter of minutes before Nina finds my bunk. That doesn't leave much I can think about, which is terrific because I'm much too tired for anything. I sit on the edge of my bed and stare into middle distance. That sounds better than it is because at this second, middle distance happens to be filled with Dena Joyce. She's just breezed into the bunk a bundle of excitement. At least someone has something to be happy about.

"I've been looking all over for you," she says, with a smile that almost touches her earlobes.

"What's up?" I can't even get past a whisper.

"I want to hear all about it."

"What?"

"Lunch."

I can't believe her. I'm so stunned I'm speechless.

"Where's your sense of humor?" she wants to know.

"Cool it, D.J., she doesn't need that," Alexandra says, following her into the bunk.

Dena Joyce gives Al a killer look, shrugs her shoulders, and wiggles off. "I didn't know we had such a delicate flower among us."

"She can be a real asshole sometimes," Alexandra says, sitting down next to me. "Think of it this way. Now you've got no place to go but up."

"Oh, yes I do."

"Where?"

"Home."

"Come on, Victoria, it's just a bad first day. You'll get the hang of it by tomorrow."

"I don't even know if I can do dinner tonight. Maybe they won't let me. Gosh, that's the first happy thought I've had since lunch."

"You'll see, dinner will be much better."

But she's wrong. Dinner is just as bad, maybe worse. I'm not even going to describe it. All I can say is that creamed spinach is even harder to scrape off than clam chowder. It got it on three people's shoulders. The fourth, Anna, my enemy, was so nervous that she made me serve her from across the table. She saved her shoulders, but when she reached for the bowl, she missed. You can't grab creamed spinach; there's nothing to hang on to. Of course I felt terrible, but not as bad as the afternoon; now that I know I'm going home.

I've decided to call my parents as soon as dinner is over and make arrangements to go home. I might even be able to get out before breakfast tomorrow morning.

"Steffi," I tell her, when we're walking back to the bunk alone after the dinner disaster, "I can't do it."

"Sure you can." She starts to give me a pep talk, but I cut her off.

"I'm going home."

She's shocked. "You can't."

"I have to."

"Just because you had a bad first day. That doesn't mean anything. Come on, Torrie. Gosh, I never thought you'd be a . . ."

"A what? A quitter?"

"Hey, I didn't mean that."

"Sure you did, and you're right, but I can't help it. It's just one of the things I can't do. Like play the violin or eat liver. I just can't do it."

"I feel awful. I mean it was going to be such a great summer, but if you're not here . . . well, it just won't be the same."

"You still have Robbie."

"But that's different. You're my best friend. Besides, we all planned to be together this summer, the three of us, didn't we?"

"I'm really sorry, Steffi, but I just can't do it."

"You could give it a little more time, couldn't you?"

I shake my head no.

I hate to do this to Steffi, but I've made up my mind. I guess she senses that because instead of getting angry, she just sort of gives up, and we walk the rest of the way in silence.

When we get to the bunk she stops, and in a very understanding voice tells me we're still best friends and if this is what I have to do, I have to do it.

The best time to catch my parents home is around 10:30. Even if they've gone out to dinner they'll be home by then. I try until 11:00, but no luck. You're not allowed to use the phone after that so I have to wait until the morning.

It's the first night I get a good night's sleep. Sure, I know it's tough on Steffi and I really do care about her, but I can't hack it. That's all. You gotta know when to stop.

I try my parents first thing in the morning. No answer. It's very strange for them to be out of the house at 6:30 in the morning. The only explanation is that they're away for a couple of days. Maybe they stayed out on Long Island with friends. My heart sinks when I think that I'll have to stay here another day. Three more meals. Three more disasters. I'll never make it.

To make matters worse, guess who's waiting for me when I get back to the bunk? That's right, El Creepo, the sister you love to lose, and her new friend, Nance. I thought I was too lucky. I avoided her for almost twenty-four hours.

"Hi, Victoria," Nina says, smiling at me as if she were some wonderful surprise.

I control myself.

"Yeah, hi," I say, and start hurrying to get into my waitress uniform.

"This is my friend, Nance. She's in my bunk."

"Hi, Nance." I give her a quick smile.

Everyone is dressed already. I can't take a chance on being late, but I don't want Nina to get suspicious. "Mommy didn't say she was going away for a couple of days, did she?"

"Yeah, she did. They went up to see somebody in Woodstock."

"Who?" I try to make it sound like just general curiosity.

"I can't remember."

"Didn't she tell you?"

"Yes, but I forgot. I didn't recognize the name." She's already opening my cubby and checking out my wardrobe. As she opens it, I close it. That doesn't stop her. She opens it again.

"What if I really needed her?" I say, slamming the door.

"Why didn't you write it down, dummy?"

"You don't have to call me names. I didn't know you needed it."

"I don't, I'm just curious."

"So?"

"What do you mean, 'so'?"

"So, what difference does it make? Besides I did write it down."

"Why didn't you say so?"

"You didn't ask."

Nina and I are so wrapped up in this dumb conversation that I don't even notice that everyone has stopped everything and is just standing there watching us. Somehow my sister brings out the worst in me. I never act this dumb with anyone else.

"Forget the whole thing," I tell her and everyone else. I'm really a little annoyed. Especially at Steffi. She shouldn't be doing this. "Just get the number and forget the whole thing."

"Huh?"

This is so baffling to everyone that they lose interest.

"Did you bring your blue vest?" Out comes the true reason for the visit.

"Of course I did."

"I told you," she says to her friend, and goes right for my cubby. "Wait till you see it. It's fabulous, exactly the same."

"Okay," I say, "so you get the number and meet me at the office."

"What number?"

"The phone number. Where Mommy and Daddy are."

"You said you didn't need it. Are you going to call them?"

"Did you show Nance the vest?"

"She has one just like it."

"So you want to borrow mine so you can dress alike?"

"Yeah, would you lend it?" Nina doesn't have to look that stunned. I lend her a lot of stuff, only most of the time I don't know I'm doing it.

"Sure. Take it and meet me with the number at the office, right?"

She knows something's up with the phone number, but she's getting the vest so she doesn't push her luck.

"I'll see you in five minutes, okay?" And she and Nancy and the vest rush out the door.

I try my parents at the number Nina gives me, but

there's no answer there either. I'll try later.

Somehow I got lucky with the lineup and flag-raising. They didn't miss me so I skip the whole thing and go straight on to the Mess Hall.

It's true, it's easier to set up the tables today, but then that wasn't my big problem. I'm okay until the people come, then I fall apart.

And here they come, hordes of them. I never thought I would feel so ugly about little kids, but they terrify me now. They are kind of cute the way they rush into the dining hall. It's so important when you're that age to have the right seat. Everyone seems to get his seat, at least the one he wants, except for Henry, the sad little boy from yesterday. He looks like his heart is going to break today.

"Hi, Henry," I say, to try to cheer him up, but it doesn't work.

"Hello," he says, and puts his head down as if he's hiding from sight.

Meanwhile, just as one of the other little boys was about to take the seat next to Henry, a bigger boy whispers something in his ear. They both look at Henry and giggle. This touches off a ripple down one side of the table. Raoul, the counselor, stops it with a stern look at the boys. Too late, it's obvious that Henry is what's so funny, and he sinks deeper into his chair, his face cherry-colored.

The bigger boy, who is obviously the leader, or the bully, puts his fingers to his nose like something smells bad, and the table falls into hysterics. It's obvious who smells. Even Raoul can't stop it this time. In fact, the more he tries the

98

louder the laughter grows. The little rats. Boy, kids really are mean sometimes.

I'm about to go over to Big Shot and drop something on his head. The way I serve, nobody would think I did it on purpose. I'm halfway around the table when Henry jumps up and races across the dining room and out the front door.

"I'll get him," I tell Raoul, and shoot out after him.

He doesn't go far. There he is, sitting on the bench in the far corner of the porch, crying.

"Henry?" I come up and put my hand on his shoulder. He's sobbing so hard I can feel his whole body shaking. "Hey, he's just a dumb bully. You can't pay any attention to him."

The same second I'm saying these things to Henry, I know how dumb I sound. He can't not pay attention to him. Everyone else does. Sure, he's a bully and he's a jerk, but so what, it still hurts. I'd cry, too.

"Can I help you?" I ask him.

He doesn't stop crying, he just shakes his head, no.

"I know how you feel," I say.

That makes him stop crying for a second. He looks up surprised. "You wet your bed, too?"

"Not anymore, but there are other things just as bad."

"No there isn't," and he's back to crying.

"What do you think about a grownup like me screwing up on a job that everyone else in the world can do with one hand tied behind her back? Didn't you see the whole place laughing at me yesterday when I dropped all those things?"

"I wanna go home," Henry sobs out to me. "Please ask them if I can go home. I don't like it here anymore."

"You're only just starting. It's a great camp and you're going to have a fabulous summer. You've just got to give it a chance."

"I wanna go home."

"You can't let a dummy like that ruin your whole summer."

"I wanna go home."

"Would you like me to talk to him? I can think of a few things that would make him think twice before he bothered you again. Would you like that?"

He shakes his head no, and tears sprinkle all over my shirt.

"What *do* you want?"

"I wanna go home."

"You can't."

"How come if I wanna?"

"Because that's quitting. And you can't quit before you really give it a try." I sound very adult and reasonable. "For starters," I say, "do you have to wet your bed?"

"Yeah."

"Okay, then we'll have to work around that. Look, Henry, there are other ways to deal with a rat like what's his name . . ."

"Steven."

". . . Steven. I love to really nail those people. Don't you worry, I'll help you."

The minute the words pop out of my mouth I remember that I'm not going to be here myself since I'm quitting, too.

Doing exactly what I'm telling Henry not to do. But of course, my situation is different.

So I go on. "You can't let bullies like that win so easily. At least go down fighting. What do you think? You want to give it a try?"

"I wanna go home."

"If you quit now, you'll always be a quitter. That's the way you'll think of yourself."

Suddenly he's stopped crying, and he's looking at me hard.

"I don't want to be a quitter."

I don't either. How come I didn't see what I'm doing until I tell some little kid?

"Neither do I," I tell him, "and that's just what I was going to do, too. Just because I had one lousy day and the worst problem imaginable with my best friend that will probably destroy our friendship. I also hate this gross creature in my bunk who always picks on me. Boy, Henry, your damp sheets don't hold a candle to all my problems."

"Then let's both go home."

I guess he's a sensible little boy, but I know that's the wrong thing to do. My dad always says you can't be a quitter.

"I'll make you a deal," I tell him. "If you stay, I'll stay."

He thinks about it for a long minute.

"Come on, Henry, we can beat them. Let's give it a try. What do you say?"

"Okay, but you gotta drop something on his head."

"I can't do that."

"Sure you can, you always do."

He's beginning to sound like Dena Joyce. Maybe he's not so cute. "Okay," I tell him, "you come back into the dining room and I'll see what I can do."

He smiles for the first time. Add no front teeth to the bedwetting. He's got a way to go.

I motion for him to follow me. "Watch out, Steven!"

"And that gross girl . . ."

"Dena Joyce."

"Dena Joyce!"

And we head into the Mess Hall, heads high, shoulders back. By the time we hit the table Henry's head is hanging again and everyone is screaming for their food.

I get so busy trying to catch up that I forget to dump on Steven. Lucky for me, I trip over the back of one of the chairs and a fried egg pops off the plate and lands smack on his head. The whole table breaks up. I wink at Henry. It's a small victory.

"Victoria Martin." The gravel voice of Madame Katzoff wipes the smile off my face. "That'll cost you fifty cents. You better shape up. And fast! Or else!" she says as she passes my tables.

It's not quitting if you get fired. But I can't do that now. I have to stick around for Henry. We made a deal. I apologize, but she doesn't even wait to acknowledge me. Steven's so deep into his fried egg that he doesn't even get the satisfaction of watching me get zonked. Well, it was worth it, and I think it helped Henry a little. At least he knows he has a friend.

Even though I'm still the last one to finish serving, it seems a little better than yesterday's breakfast. Not as much improvement as I think, though, when I remember that I didn't serve breakfast yesterday. My disaster started with lunch.

"Torrie," Steffi says, poking her head back into the dining room, "we'll wait for you on the porch, okay?"

I would love to say no, but there's no way. I can't avoid my best friend every time she's with her boyfriend. She's sure to catch on pretty fast.

"I'll be out in a minute," I call back. I have to pull myself together for this. Just the sight of Robbie shakes me up so much that I'm sure everybody can see. And that would be horrendous—if Steffi knew, I mean.

I can see them through the screen door. They're sitting at the far end of the porch, very close on the wooden bench. And they're talking. It all looks very private, so I decide to just wait. And wait.

Obviously they could do this forever, so I cough a few times to give them warning, groan, shove the screen door open, and go out onto the porch.

"Hi, Steffi," I say very up and looking only at Steffi. "Hi, Robbie." Still up and only looking at Steffi. I don't think I can carry this off.

"That was pretty fast," Steffi says, trying to look on the bright side. "You're really getting into it."

Now Robbie tries his helping hand. "It's only ten minutes extra. That's not too bad, you know, ten minutes."

"Yeah," I say, looking over his head. "Ten minutes later than Claire and all the other retards. Great."

"Well, it's only for another day or so, right? When are they going to pick you up or what?"

"They're not going to. I changed my mind."

Steffi jumps up and hugs me. "That's fabulous! Oh, I'm so happy. Now it's going to be a perfect summer. The three of us. That's the way it's going to be!"

Ugh!

"That's great," Robbie says. "Steffi really felt terrible about your going home. So did I."

I don't even look on his side of the porch for that one.

"What happened?" Steffi wants to know.

"I just thought some more about it and decided that I would give it another chance. One day isn't enough, I guess." If Robbie weren't around I would tell Steffi the truth about Henry and quitting, but with Robbie here I just feel strange. I can't be myself. In fact, I struggle just to speak regular. It's going to be one long horrendous summer.

"Let's all get a Coke, okay, Robbie?" Steffi says.

"I can't, Stef," he says. "I have to be down at the waterfront in about ten minutes. Want to walk me down?"

"Sure," Steffi says. "How about it, Torrie? You haven't even seen the waterfront yet, have you?"

"I'll go down this afternoon," I lie, because I intend never to go. At least not while Robbie's on duty, and that's probably all the time, since he's in charge of the waterfront.

"Come on, Torrie, you got time."

"I can't." Another lie. "I promised Nina that I would stop by and see her bunk."

Steffi gives me a funny look. That was dumb—she knows me too well.

"Okay," she says, "I'll catch you back at the bunk."

And she and Robbie go off toward the lake. I stand there on the porch, alone. I feel terrible. The most important friendship in my life is going down the tubes, and I can't stop it.

Let's face it, I'm just like Steffi—madly in love with Robbie. And something else. Is it my imagination, or is he beginning to give me strange looks? Nice strange. Too nice strange.

What a mess!

I don't want to look like too much of a liar, so I stop by Nina's bunk. Lucky for me it's empty. I take back my vest, which of course is thrown on the floor in true Nina slob way. By the time I get back to my own bunk, good old D.J. is there.

"Lucky you," she says.

"How come?" I say, probably falling into the biggest trap ever made.

"You pulled dock duty for all of next week. Don't look so innocent. You may fool your dear best friend, but I'm a lot smarter."

"Hey, gimme a break, huh? I don't even know what you're talking about."

Just as I say it, I realize what she's talking about. Robbie runs the waterfront. I have to be his assistant for seven days. I can't do it. That's all. I just can't do it.

"If you think it's so sensational, we can switch, then you can be the lucky one."

"I think Mr. Robbie Wagner is absolutely adorable. A real hot ticket. But not worth a week of shivering in a wet bathing suit. No thanks, you keep it."

"Maybe Claire . . ."

"Are you kidding? She hates the water worse than I do. Why don't you ask dear old Steffi? I'm sure she'd love to switch places to be near her boyfriend. If she was smart she would."

"I don't even know why I talk to you about this anyway. You've got such a warped view of everything. Robbie is my best friend's boyfriend, period."

"Sure thing," she says, giving me that sly nasty smile.

I wonder about people like Dena Joyce. She must like being mean. I wonder if there's anyone she would be nice to. So far I haven't seen any sign of niceness. And I'm finished trying to be nice to her—from now on I'm going to treat her like she deserves. Let her say one more thing to me, and I'm going to really sock it to her. Just one more thing.

And she does. "Hey, Victoria, you got the time?"

"Bug off, will you?" I answer, just as Claire, Alexandra, and one of the twins come into the bunk. So everyone thinks I'm nuts. So what?

Staying was a dumb idea. It can only get worse. I should have minded my own business with Henry and I would have been set to go home right this minute.

"Anybody want to switch dock duty for anything you want?" I ask generally. Nobody answers. "I'll exchange for anything." I look at Claire.

"Who wouldn't?" Claire says, rolling her eyes. "That's the worst job around."

"Claire's right," one of the twins says. "Everyone's got

to do it, so I don't think it's fair for anyone to get out of it."

"If someone wants to change with me, it's my business. Besides, I was just asking."

"Well," twinny says, "I'm saying no."

"Fine. Anyone else?"

Only Alexandra is nice about it, but she loves what she has, arts and crafts, so she doesn't want to change. So far I'm stuck, and everyone thinks I'm just trying to get out of a hard job. Maybe Steffi wants to change. I have to be careful. She'd probably think I can't stand to be near him for a whole week. Boy, is she right, but for all the wrong reasons.

When Steffi and I are walking to the Mess Hall, I tell her I would be willing to change dock duty next week if she likes, and then she could spend a whole extra week with Robbie.

"Oh, I'd love to but I don't think I can get out of Drama Group. Becky Walker specially requested me for the first week to help organize the summer program. I was very involved last year. I already said yes, but an extra week with Robbie is so tempting . . ." Steffi is really struggling. Finally, she says she can't.

Unless I can think of something brilliant over the weekend I'm stuck for dock duty starting Monday.

I make one last try with the other twin on Sunday, but she's not interested either. Somehow Steffi finds out that I've been trying to dump the assignment, and of course she thinks it's because I don't like Robbie.

"That's not true, Steffi," I tell her. "It's just that I'm going to get my period next week and I hate to be stuck in a bathing suit."

She buys it, but that's not great. Now I have to pretend to have my period all next week and pretend not to have it the following week when I really will have it. This whole thing gets worse by the minute. A week of dock duty. Horrendous. I'll never make it.

7

Monday morning starts like all Monday mornings—rain. Well, not exactly rain, just slight drizzle. The light gray kind of day that looks like it might clear up any minute. Just promising enough to keep the people on dock duty at their stations.

Alone.

That's just what I needed—to be alone with Robbie. Of course he's very friendly, welcoming me, showing me around and explaining rules like how we handle the safety equipment and all that. I force myself to pay close attention because it's serious business, but half my brain is stuck on thinking how handsome he is close up and how much I like the sound of his voice. Every once in a while I forget and look up at his face, at his bottom lip, especially, when he smiles. He's got the sweetest smile, with just a trace of a dimple on one cheek. I guess I knew all this from Steffi, but I never knew what it would make me feel like. It makes me feel like I want to reach out and touch him.

And when we do touch, accidentally, the feeling ripples through my body and I get warm all over. How am I going to last seven days? That thought almost makes me want to cry.

I find a little trick that helps. Whenever I get too carried away, lost in the sound of his voice or the sight of that bottom lip, I say, "Steffi." That's it, I just say her name over and over again like it's some kind of magic charm that will break the spell.

When I run out of charms I just clam up. At first he chats with me, the way you would with someone you're working with, but all I can manage are one-syllable answers so the conversation just kind of dribbles away. Then it gets silent, and that's hard to break. It's obvious he thinks I don't like him, but that's the price I have to pay.

One bad thing happens in the morning. The two of us are out there reading, about ten feet apart, when a frog croaks and we both look up at the same instant. For a second neither of us realizes that we're staring at each other.

It's intense, the way our eyes get locked together for that moment. Finally, I force myself back to the book, but that's it; I can't read another thing for the rest of the morning.

The afternoon is just as horrendous. At about 3:00 Steffi comes down to visit us, and I feel so guilty I can't even look at her. I haven't *done* one thing wrong, but everything I *think* is horrible.

And she doesn't have much luck with Robbie, either. I guess just sitting around here in this funny kind of gloom has hit him, too.

Steffi pulls me aside. "What's up? Are you both in the dumps or what?"

"It's just the weather. It's really depressing to sit around here in this drizzle."

But she doesn't buy my explanation. "Look, I know you're not crazy about Robbie, but at least you could try to be a little friendly . . ."

"That's not fair, Steffi. It's really hard. Here we are alone all this time and we barely know each other."

"I guess you're right, Torrie, I'm sorry. It's just that it's so important to me that you two like each other. Maybe I'm pushing too hard."

"Yeah, it just takes time."

By now Robbie has finished checking the lines and we're all back together. It's awful-time again.

"What do you think?" he says. "Is it going to clear up?"

We do the weather bit for a few minutes, and then I find an excuse to leave them alone.

They walk over to the end of the dock and talk. I watch them. She loves him: I can see that. I can see it in her eyes, in her face, in the way she moves close to him and touches his arm whenever she can. I hope she can't see it in me.

They talk for a while, then he bends down and kisses her lightly on her forehead. When he straightens up he looks in my direction.

I look away. Why did he do that? There's something strange about his attitude toward me. I'm not sure if it's just me seeing him through my feelings or if he really is acting different.

Finally, after a hundred years, Steffi goes back to her drama group. Great how I love to get rid of my best friend, isn't it?

The rest of the afternoon is spent in serious silence. The weather's getting worse, drippy and chilly, but I'm not even cold. In fact, I'm practically in a sweat.

At 5:00 we say goodbye and he goes in one direction and I go in another. Intense.

Tuesday is a total nightmare. Between waitressing and dock duty, my life is an awesome disaster. We are now, that's Robbie and me, at the point where we don't talk at all. When he comes around to my side of the dock, I smile nicely and walk around to the other side. If he does ask me something, I practically jump out of my skin at the sound of his voice.

By the way, it's drizzling again. All day.

I spend the afternoon in dread of Steffi's visit. That's the worst time. It's very tricky because we both have to come up with all sorts of crazy things that make us look busy. I must have tied the knot on the line to the raft ten times. The last time I do it I'm trying so hard to look involved that I forget what I'm doing, and the minute I turn my back it opens, the rope slides off the dock, and the raft is free.

Nothing to do but go in after it. It may be cold and awful, but it's better than facing Steffi.

It comes to me sometime during the hours I spend sitting, damp and shivering, trying to concentrate on the book I've been staring at for the last two days: summer camp is like a prison sentence.

And I feel like a criminal, too, trying to steal my best friend's boyfriend. That's the truth. Sure, I'm not doing it outright, but I love him, and inside my heart, I want him to love me, too.

At night, I don't take part in any of the activities. I say I'm not feeling well. Steffi thinks I have my period, so she accepts it. Maybe she doesn't accept it completely, but she wants to, so that helps. Besides, she spends a lot of time with Robbie now.

The only one of the other girls I'm friendly with is Alexandra. Liza is okay, but just not my type, and I couldn't care less about the twins. Claire is a dodo and I outright hate and despise Dena Joyce.

"How's dock duty?" D.J. asks every chance she gets. And the way she says it is so nasty that I'm afraid Steffi will notice. For some reason she doesn't. It's like she's oblivious. Why shouldn't she be? Would she suspect her best friend of betraying her? Of course not.

Meanwhile, Ken is around a lot. I don't give him any encouragement, but then I know why he's hanging around. He wants to be near Steffi. She's so dense about anyone but Robbie that she doesn't even notice, except to say how nice he is and how much he likes me.

"Why don't we all go down for a soda?" he asks me, staring at Steffi.

"I'm going to pass," I say. "I'm too tired. Thanks anyway."

"How about you, Steffi?" He's practically drooling.

"Only if Victoria wants to. I'm sort of tired myself."

Now he's got to turn back to me. I never saw such pleading in anyone's eyes. How can I say no? I'm such a horrendous person lately that I better grab my one little chance to be nice to someone.

"Okay," I say, "I'll go."

He practically kisses me. Naturally Steffi in her great denseness whispers to me that he's out-of-his-mind-happy that I'm going. I don't even bother to tell her the truth.

When we get down to the Rec Hall, the music is blasting, and it's jammed. Everybody is there.

But not Robbie, thank goodness. For the first time since I arrived, or more accurately since he arrived, I'm having a good time. I love to dance and I'm pretty good at it, so I get asked a lot. Nobody really sends me wild, but it's fun, and I even have a good time with Steffi.

"This is great," she says to me. "You're like your old self again."

"I think I got a second wind."

I dance with Ken a couple of times, but he only has eyes for Steffi. They really get along pretty well. If Robbie weren't in the picture they'd make a good couple. But Robbie is not only in the picture; when I turn around to get a cold drink, he's also there in the flesh. We see each other and turn away quickly. I'm back where I started. My evening is ruined.

Rather than start making up reasons why I'm suddenly back to gloom-face, I whisper to Steffi that I'm really exhausted and I'm going back to the bunk. She's disappointed, but understands. I get out before she sees Robbie, so there's no way for her to connect his coming with my going.

When I get back to the bunk there's a message from my

parents asking me to call them. It's still early enough, so I hurry down to the front office and phone them.

"How's it going, honey?" my dad asks.

"Great," I tell him.

"What's wrong?"

How can they always tell so fast? "Nothing. It's just it's a lot harder than I thought."

"Maybe I should have told you about the time I worked as a waiter at the Carnegie Deli in New York. What a mess. I dropped a tray loaded with pickles and mustard all over a customer who turned out to be the owner's father-in-law."

"Oh, Daddy, now I know where I get it from. What happened? Did they fire you?"

"On the spot. But I wasn't defeated. Now I could tell everyone I was an experienced waiter. I just left out a couple of details."

"I don't even think I'll be lucky enough to get fired. I'll just end up with so many fines that I'll owe them money at the end of the summer."

"Hang in there, honey. I guarantee you're going to end up loving it."

"Hah!"

"Take my word for it," he says, and then tells me a few more things about his short but brilliant career in the restaurant business. And somehow I feel better. Nothing ever seems so horrendous after I talk to my dad.

Of course, I don't tell him about Robbie. Nobody can help me about that nightmare.

Walking back to the bunk, the air is warm and smells

delicious, like the forest after a rain. The sky is clear and filled with stars. It's supposed to be beautiful tomorrow. At least we won't have to be alone again: we have swimming groups all day, plus two general swims with the whole camp.

It's so lovely out that I take off the plastic stuff I had covering the hole in the wall behind my bed. Now I sort of have my own little porthole. I've gotten so used to the country that I don't even worry about animals crawling in and falling on my head. I figure if they don't come in through the windows, they won't come in through this little hole. That's what I figure. If I'm wrong, I'll probably have a heart attack.

Which will cure my Robbie problem, anyway. Everything always comes back to that. Because I never felt this way about anyone else before. Whenever I think about him, I say in my head, "I love you, Robbie." I say it over and over again. I'm always nervous when I'm with him because of Steffi, but if that situation didn't exist, I would want to be with him all the time. I would want to touch him and have his arms around me. I would want to kiss him, to feel his lips on mine, his body pressed against mine. The whole length of him. But it's not possible. None of it. I can control the outside, but not what I feel inside.

The next morning is magnificent, just the way it's supposed to be in summer camp. Two days of rain turned everything bright shiny green, and a million flowers bloomed. Even the shrubbery around the slum bunks looks good. Of course, if you know anything about it, you know it's all weeds, but at least they cover the broken shutters and piles of garbage.

I don't know why I'm feeling so good today. Maybe it's because of that conversation with my father, or maybe because I didn't drop anything big and wet at breakfast. Toast sliding off a plate or a runaway hard-boiled egg hardly count in my case. I'm getting better. I was out in under ten minutes. That's ten minutes after everyone else. I barely had time to think about my fantastic success, because I'm due down at the dock by nine o'clock. First group is junior girls. Nina and her friends.

There are twenty-six thirteen-year-olds. Eighteen of them claim they can't go in the water because they have their periods. They barely have the strength to drag themselves over to the grass, throw down their towels, take out their

117

suntan lotion, and start polishing their nails.

Unfortunately, Nina is one of the well ones, and she and seven others go through the life-saving lessons. For the next hour she bugs me every five minutes.

"Victoria," she calls out from the water, "is this right?" she says, doing a backstroke. Or, "Are my legs straight?" and fifty other unnecessary questions.

I don't want to look like a bad sister in front of Robbie, so I answer her as sweetly as possible. She sees what's happening and takes hideous advantage of the situation.

I would love to push her head under the water. And hold it there for about a month. All right, two weeks.

Then, right in earshot of Robbie, she asks me about Todd, and before I have a chance to answer informs me that her friend, Lisa, his sister, told her that he is definitely going out with Judy First.

I know Robbie hears that because he looks up at me for a second. Then she asks me if she can borrow my pink sweater. I would like to wrap it around her throat, but I can't seem selfish in front of Robbie, so I say yes. It nearly chokes me.

Finally, the end of first activity is announced over the PA, and they all head for their second activity.

"I'll stop by your bunk later for the sweater," Nina calls as she leaves. "Okay?"

I don't answer.

But it's not that easy with Nina. "Okay?" she shouts again.

"Yeah."

And she's gone.

The next group is Henry's. I can see them coming in the distance. They look so cute, walking in double file holding hands.

When they get close enough I smile and wave at them. I love them. They're my table.

They're all surprised to see me and maybe a little nervous. After all, if I save lives or teach swimming anything like I serve meals, they know they're in deep trouble.

Of course, I'm friendly, but I try to look sort-of professional to build up their confidence.

Robbie is really in charge of the lessons, but I have to keep a watch, too. They're six- to eight-year-olds, and you have to keep a sharp eye on them because they're always swimming away on their own or doing something crazy. In the water they're like a lot of little porpoises leaping and playing around.

Robbie lines them all up in the shallow part of the crib. That's a portion of the lake enclosed with ropes where the kids all have to swim unless they've passed their deep-water tests. When they do, they can swim out to the raft. It gets pretty deep further out in the crib. These kids are so little that they can't stand at the middle of the crib, so we have to be very careful that they don't drift away out of the beginner area. Of course, the counselors keep an eye on them, too.

Unfortunately, Henry gets put right next to his mortal enemy, the big dumb bully, Steven. I would like to change his place, but I don't want to do that without asking Robbie, and he's busy with a demonstration of the crawl.

It turns out to be okay anyway, because Henry is a better

swimmer than expected, so I don't have to worry about Steven pushing him around.

After the lesson Robbie gives them all a free swim period. The crib turns into one big splash with lots of shouting and laughing and plenty of "watch me's." That's what they all want. "Victoria, watch me!" Even Henry is having a good time. At least Steven seems to be leaving him alone.

I'm busy showing one of the younger boys, Timmy Whelan, the dead-man's float when suddenly there's a lot of commotion way down at the end of the crib.

Something's wrong! I grab Timmy, toss him up on the dock, and run down to the end of the pier to see what's happening.

When I get there I see a couple of the kids have gone under the ropes and are way out in the deep water. And they're shouting. It's serious!

I dive in and, swimming as fast as I can, head for them. It takes forever when you have to move fast in the water, but I finally get there. It turns out to be Steven and one of his little followers.

"What's wrong?" I ask them, trying to catch my breath. "What are you kids doing this far out?"

"Henry. It's Henry," the little one gasps, sputtering with water.

"Where is he?" I ask, looking all around. He's nowhere in sight. "Where is he?" I shout at Steven.

"He was over there." He points to an empty spot a few feet away toward the raft.

"Get back and get Robbie—fast!" I tell them, and dive under the water.

The lake is clean and you can see far down into the tall weeds. Streaks of sunlight cut through the water, making my air bubbles glisten as they race up behind me. There's nothing but silence and stillness and emptiness. I swing around in a full circle. No Henry. A horrendous panic shortens my breath and I have to surface to fill my lungs again. I search the top of the water. Still no Henry. Oh, please, please don't let anything awful happen to him. He's so sweet and so little.

I have to find him fast. If he *is* underwater, even seconds can be too long.

Down I dive again. This time I head toward the wooden raft. If he got into trouble he may have tried to make it to the raft. Then I see him, just off the edge of the raft. For an instant he looks okay, but then I see him sliding away from the raft and sinking down, his arms above his head, bubbles rushing from his mouth.

I shoot up from the water, take a huge gulp of air, and dive down again. Pushing the water behind me with my arms, kicking furiously, I swim down toward the spot where I estimate he should be when I get to him. I have to go deeper than I thought, and I didn't take in enough air. But I can't go up again. It would take too long. I have to keep going. It's just another couple of seconds and I'll reach him.

A hard pain fills my chest. I have to force myself to keep going down to Henry. The pain is like a steel wire tightening around me. My head feels like it's going to explode. I reach out to try to grab him, but he's still too far away. Please don't let it be too late. One more inch and I won't be able to do it. I can't stand the pain.

And then I get him. I pull him to me, wrap my arm around his body, bend my knees up, and shove my feet out with all the power in my legs. We shoot up through the water together, me holding Henry with one arm while I propel myself with the other, kicking madly all the while.

I see the top of the water . . . another couple of feet and I'll break through. But then I can't! The stopped-up air inside of me explodes out and just as quickly a rush of water gushes into my mouth, choking back any air left. In that instant, with all my might I throw Henry up as far as I can, straight up out of the water, and incredibly, hands grab him from me and then the water floods my brain and I fight for air to stop the choking. I feel myself being pushed up, my head bursts free of the water, but I can't get the air into me. I can't stop the coughing long enough to inhale. All the while choking and coughing, I'm being pulled along through the water. I know somebody's saving me, but all I care about is getting some air into my lungs. I have to breathe . . .

And then I do. Between the coughs I begin to grab a little air. It turns into choking when it gets to my lungs, but some air seeps in, and through the coughing and gasping, a little more, and some of the panic stops because I'm beginning to breathe again.

I feel myself being lifted out of the water and carried in someone's arms. My arms hang down. I'm too exhausted to even hold my head up. All I can manage is breathing.

Gently, I'm put down on the grass and for the first time I begin to breathe normally.

I open my eyes and see his face, inches from mine.

Someplace, way back inside my brain, I knew it was Robbie saving me. Something about the feel of his arms holding me, his chest against my body: I knew it was him.

And now I'm looking at him, caught in his eyes and too weak to turn away. And I see something in his face and I feel something between us, and it makes tears well up in my eyes.

"Are you okay?" he asks softly.

I shake my head yes. "Henry? Is he all right?"

"Yes," he says, gently brushing the hair back from my forehead. "You got him just in time. He's okay."

And now the tears come. I turn my head to the side, put my hands over my face, and cry. Part of it is relief for Henry and for myself, and another part is a terrible sadness for what I know is happening between Robbie and me. Something that neither of us can help.

He knows it, too. And he stays there, hovering over me a moment too long. And then he pulls himself up and others, people I didn't even see before, move in and help me up.

"Where's Henry?" I ask them. "I want to see him."

"He's over there on the bench," one of the counselors says. "Thanks to you, he's okay."

And sure enough, there he is, all wrapped in a blanket and he's just fine. I go over to him and grab him up in my arms. Boy, I was never so happy to see any kid in my life.

"You okay?" I ask, squeezing him.

"Yeah," he says, "I'm okay. You saved my life. I would of drowned. Thank you, Victoria." And with that he gives me a huge smacker on the cheek. I give him one right back and everyone laughs.

We're all feeling pretty good.

"What happened?" I ask him. "What were you doing all the way out there?"

Suddenly he gets very quiet. Something's up. He won't talk.

"Hey, you know you aren't supposed to be out of the crib until you pass your test. How come you did that?"

Henry puts his head down, and I can see he's going to cry if I bug him anymore.

"It's okay," I hug him, "but just don't do that anymore. Right?"

"I won't," he says. "I promise."

"Steven made him," Adam Gold pipes up from the back of the crowd.

I turn to look at him. "How'd he do that?"

But now Adam clams up. Suddenly he doesn't know anything. And nobody else does. I might have known Steven was involved. Boy, I could kick that kid! He really is a little shit.

I can see there's no point in trying to get the real story now. First of all, Henry's too upset, and besides, no one is going to spill it in front of a whole crowd like this. But I'm not finished with that little monster yet. No way.

Naturally, after all that, swim period is called off.

"Victoria?" It's Robbie. "Why don't you go back to your bunk and lie down for a while? I can manage okay for now."

"I'm all right, really," I tell him, but he insists, and then the JC gets in too and says I look very pale. Maybe I should stop by the infirmary. He offers to go with me.

"I'll go lie down, but I don't think I need to see the doctor. I'm really okay, just kind of wiped out."

I put on my robe and go up toward the bunks.

Nobody is in the bunk when I get there. All I want to do anyway is fall down on the bed. I'm worse than I thought. And when I think about what happened and what could have happened, I start to get sick to my stomach. I think about Henry and how he could have died. And me, too. That's how those things can happen in the water. One minute everything is okay, and you're laughing, and then the next somebody's dead. Wow! That's the closest I ever came to anything that serious.

I guess I really did save Henry's life. I remember once my parents talking about this old Chinese proverb. I don't remember the words, but it's about how when you save somebody's life, they become your responsibility for always; you're obligated to them because you gave them a new life. You're sort of their mother. Now I really have to take care of Henry.

Wait till I get my hands on that rotten little Steven.

I guess I fell asleep, because the next thing I know the PA is blasting dinner call. They must have let me sleep through the setup. I jump up, throw on my uniform, and race down to the Mess Hall.

Steffi sees me coming in the door and comes right over to me and gives me a huge hug. "You're fabulous, Torrie. Everybody's talking about how you saved Henry's life. You're terrific."

125

And then a million other people are crowding around me and hugging me and congratulating me, and it's terrific. It's like I'm a hero. It's great.

Turns out all the waitresses got together and were sharing my tables so I could rest. I look at my tables, and for the first time they're eating at the same time as everyone else.

I thank everyone and take over my station. In a few minutes it's like usual. They're one course behind. They all say they're used to it and besides they like the leisurely pace.

Just before dessert, both my tables stand up and give me a cheer, and then the whole dining room applauds. Boy, am I glad I stayed.

For the next week and a half I live off the big rescue, but by the end of the second week nobody's talking about it anymore. The high is gone, and I'm back down in the dumps again. Henry, too. It's tough for both of us. He's been trying, but he hasn't had much success yet. He still walks around looking like he just lost his last friend, which isn't possible since he never had any to start with, and he still cries at least five times a day and looks just plain unhappy the rest of the time. Plus, he's still king of the damp sheets. In fact, the only success he's had is with me. I stayed because of him. And I hate it. Some success.

Most of the time I feel about as miserable as Henry looks. The big three problems are still big and three—Robbie, Steffi, and pain-in-the-ass Dena Joyce.

My heart is still doing those crazy jumps when I see Robbie, and I can never carry on a decent conversation when he's around. So mostly I just stay quiet and study him. I'm beginning to see more of the person inside.

A couple of days ago, a whole group of us were watching the weekly tennis meets. They had three matches going on at the same time, but most everyone was watching Robbie and this fabulous player Wally Kramer. Wally is a notorious bad sport with the most horrendous temper; he's the kind who smashes rackets if he loses. And he was really going bananas that day because Robbie was holding his own against him. Every time he lost a point Wally had something nasty to say.

At one point they were neck and neck with Wally serving. He has this fantastic serve that's like a bullet and nobody can ever return it, but this time he overshot the line. Robbie called it out and everybody saw it was, but Wally blew up, threw his racket down, and really got crazed.

By then Robbie had had it. "Hey, Kramer, you got a problem? Say it, don't do a whole number."

"Yeah, well, I don't like your calls."

"Okay, then, let's forget the whole thing," Robbie said, and started to walk off. That's when Wally called after him, something about first you cheat and then you quit, and Robbie turned around, and in two seconds he was over the net and they were rolling around on the ground. It was wild how fast it all happened.

They stopped it before it got very far, but even Steffi was surprised. Somehow you don't think of Robbie as the type to lose his temper like that. It's not that he was really wrong, Wally is definitely a crud, and you can't just go around calling people cheaters and get away with it. Still Robbie always seemed so cool and under control; it was weird to see him like that.

Mostly I know about Robbie from Steffi, and she never says anything bad about him. I guess nobody can be that perfect, but you wouldn't know it from Steffi's description. She can go on forever about how brilliant he is, and how he just started Stanford and he's at the top of his class already, and how he's a fabulous athlete and so unspoiled even though he comes from this ultra-rich family in Connecticut.

Ken Irving isn't so crazy about him, but that's probably because he likes Steffi. He says Robbie's a little too sure of himself. Maybe he's just jealous. Most of the other guys like him, and the girls certainly do. If it weren't for Steffi, there'd probably be a stampede to get at him.

I guess there are lots of things about Robbie Wagner that are just plain regular person, still there's a lot about him that's different. He's sort of aloof, and I like that. Like when the other guys are roughhousing and fooling around, he doesn't get involved. They're all about the same age, but he seems more sophisticated. That appeals to me, too. Most of the boys I know are still at the goofy stage. It's like he passed it already, except that fight business. That was really out of character—very immature.

"That was very immature," D.J. says to Steffi and me later in the bunk.

It's okay if I think it, but it bugs me to hear D.J. say it.

"I don't think so." I'm dumb enough to fall for the bait. "Wally Kramer is pure nerd city."

"Asshole is more like it," Steffi adds, "and it's time someone stopped him."

"Oh, dear, Robbie and his girlfriends." And with a hideous wink at me, D.J. wiggles off.

"She gives me such a pain," Steffi says. "One of these

days I'm really going to let her have it."

"Forget it, she's just jealous."

"How come you're so nice about her lately? She's such a shit."

"I just tune her out."

What I don't tell Steffi is that I hate D.J. even more than she does, but I'm in no position to start any kind of trouble with her. All I have to do is give her one little piece of ammunition and she'll blow my whole friendship with Steffi to smithereens.

As is, we're only okay when we're alone, and even then there's a tiny something that's not quite right. As long as she doesn't know what it is, it's okay; I can put up with it. I think she thinks I'm just not completely happy here at camp, and since she's the one who talked me into going, she doesn't want to push it too much.

Besides, in a little more than a week the summer will be half over. Not a minute too soon for me. What a disaster!

Actually, it's not a total bomb. For one thing, the bunk turned out to be okay. Nobody inspects us, so we can keep it the way we want, which means you can't tell the garbage heap outside from the one inside. There isn't one neat person in the whole bunk. That's really lucky, because I think she would have killed herself or the rest of us by now.

There never was enough room in the cubbies or the closet in the back, but somehow, in the beginning, everything fit better. Now, you can't find the cubbies for all the clothes thrown around. Beds have not been made in weeks, and sheets aren't changed unless something drastic is spilled on them. Actually, it's heaven. We all love it. It's like living the way you always dreamed. And you don't even have to feel guilty, because everyone else is just as bad as you are.

Only one problem. Don't ever misplace anything, because you will never find it.

There's only one cleaning job we all do. Soda cans. If you don't take them out at night, by the next morning the entire ant population of the Western Hemisphere finds them. And they march right in the front door. The first time we made that mistake, actually it was D.J., she shoved her empty can under Claire's bed. Naturally, she wouldn't do it under her own. Claire, jerk that she is, probably thanked her. Anyway, the next morning there was a six-inch-wide wavy black line moving across the room connecting the door to the soda can. Four billion ants had come for the party.

Alexandra and the twins cleaned them up while the rest of us stood around screaming, squealing in horror and disgust and rushing around shaking out all the piles of clothes on the floor. The poor ants were probably frightened to death.

From then on: no empty soda cans allowed. Anything nonfood can stay on the floor—permanently.

This all proves that our parents are completely wrong. There's no harm in sloppiness. Other than some wrinkled clothes, it's perfectly fine. And if you lose something in the mess you're bound to find it when you pack to go home.

I've made a good friend of Alexandra. The twins aren't so awful, except they never do anything alone and they agree with whoever gets to them first. Liza is fun in small doses. Claire is hopeless, and D.J. is like a wicked witch in training.

And there's no way to avoid her. She's always watching me, waiting for me to make a mistake. But she's in for a surprise—I'm not going to. All I got to do is stay loose for twenty-six days and I've got it made. It's a cinch. That's what I keep telling myself.

I wish I could really believe it.

We're all waiting for *Color War* to break. *Color War* is a special thing that happens only in summer camp. It's a kind of big competition. The camp is divided into two teams, the green team and the gray. Then you do all the regular field sports, only you play for your team. After three days the team with the most points wins. There are also special events, like play night and sing night. Each team puts on an original musical, and the best one wins a lot of points. Everything is divided into teams, even arts and crafts, and then certain counselors judge the winners.

If you're on the green team you have to wear green all the time. And except for when you go back to the bunk to dress or sleep, you always stay with your teammates, even when you march to meals or anything.

You can see what a big deal all of this is. It gets to be very important, and you really go all out for your team. Anyway, you never know how *Color War* is going to break. It's always very exciting. Steffi told me that last year they had a small plane fly over the campus and drop leaflets announcing *Color War* and giving lists of team members.

One night, Steffi, Alexandra, and I are sitting around hanging out when I get the idea, wouldn't it be fun to break Color War ourselves.

At first we're all just kidding around, but it begins to kind of grow and before you know it we put together the whole thing. It doesn't sound hard, and it would really be a gas. All we need is some green and gray crepe paper.

The plan is to wait until everyone is asleep, then sneak into the bunks and tie either a green or gray piece of paper to the end of each bed. When the kids get up in the morning, they'll all think Color War has started. It would be fabulous. No one has ever done such a thing before.

I have Thursday morning off so I go into town to get the crepe paper. We plan to break it just before the weekend.

It's imperative that Dena Joyce and Claire the squealer not know what we're planning.

This means that we have to hide the paper until Friday night. The best place to keep it is where it belongs. No one would ever look for it there.

We plan to do it around three or four in the morning. The three of us will sneak out of our bunk and each one will take one row of bunks to do.

I get the last row, that's seniors and intermediates, the oldest kids.

Steffi doesn't even tell Robbie, and on Friday night we leave the dance early and go back to the bunk to get everything ready.

Before the others get back we set everything up, hiding black T-shirts and jeans in our beds under the covers so that we can change into them when the lights are out. We each put our supply of crepe paper in the beds, too. We cut the strips into short pieces the right size to tie around the metal footboards of the beds. Each one takes a mixture of gray and green.

Alexandra has an alarm watch that she sets for 3:30. She hardly has to bother, since I'm so excited that I can't sleep a wink anyway.

Funny to watch other people sleep. Dena Joyce, the one we really have to worry about, changes positions every three minutes. I've never seen such a restless sleeper.

I keep an eye on my watch, and just before three I wake up Alexandra so that she can turn off her alarm before it goes off.

"Huh?" she says, totally dazed.

"Shush . . . it's time to get up."

Then I wake Steffi, who's just as groggy, and the three of us tiptoe out of the bunk.

"It's pitch-black," Steffi whispers to me.

And it is. It's a new moon, which is no moon at all. I never could understand who made that one up. Why not just say no-moon and not make people crazy? Anyway, it's a no-moon, and the only lights around are the tree lights and there aren't many of those, so we're really in the dark.

It's a little better when your eyes get used to it and, of course, we know our own bunk.

I push open the screen door and it squeaks. We stop dead, but nobody seems to have heard. Quickly the three of us slip out onto the porch. We'd be in big trouble if this wasn't our bunk, but luckily we know how to avoid the broken places in the flooring.

"What do you think?" Steffi asks us.

Alexandra's answer is a big gulping sound. That's exactly the way I feel, too. Scared. It sounded like such a fun idea when we were sitting around planning it but now—it's turned scary. If they catch us we're really finished. And there are a million ways for this to go wrong. If somebody wakes and sees us they'll probably scream. I can just see that, one kid screaming and then all the others wake up and start screaming, too. What if they think we're thieves? They could even attack us.

"You want to forget it?" I ask them.

"Oh, no," Alexandra says, shaking her head furiously, "absolutely not. No way . . . unless, of course, you want to . . ."

"Uh-uh," I say.

". . . or maybe Steffi?" You can tell she'd love Steffi to say no.

But Steffi says she's not going to be the one to chicken out.

"Me neither," says Alexandra, and then to me, "and you certainly can't since it was your idea."

"I wouldn't dream of it." For the first time I'm not so crazy about Alexandra. It's easy to see that none of us wants to do it. It's funny, but we're all stuck.

"Should we vote on it?" I take one last chance.

"What's the point of a vote if no one is disagreeing?" Al asks.

"I just want to be democratic."

"Okay," she says, "anybody for chickening out?"

We all raise our hands. And then we break up laughing.

"Come on," Steffi says, "we have to do it. It's such a fabulous idea."

"We got past the worst part already," Alexandra says.

"How's that?" I ask.

"What's worse than Dena Joyce?"

"It's settled," I say, "let's move it."

And the three of us go off into the black night, each one of us heading for a different row.

The minute I leave them my knees begin to buckle. The idea of doing this is scary enough but the idea of doing it alone is absolutely terrifying. Next time I'll keep my big mouth shut.

The first bunk is the oldest girls, Superseniors. They're fifteen. I know most of them because they're sort of in our group. At least, they're invited to our parties.

I get out seven pieces of crepe paper, put my shopping bag down, and carefully and quietly creep up the steps to bunk five. It's all quiet. I turn the doorknob and gently open the screen door. It's nearly pitch-black. I slip into the room as silently as I can and tiptoe over to the first bed. Carefully I tie a piece of the paper around the metal bar at the foot of the bed. I get the second one ready.

I tie that one on. Nobody wakes up. This must be what it's like to be a thief. It's horrible and I'm a wreck, and this is only my first bunk. I'll never make it.

But I do. At least I finish the first bunk. I have no idea how many of each color I did. It was too dark. But it doesn't make any difference anyway.

By the third bunk I'm like a professional. It's incredible how soundly everyone sleeps. I'm beginning to get excited because it's going to work. Then I start to get giggly. I can feel it growing in the bottom of my stomach which is ridiculous since I'm all alone, but I can't help myself.

I tie on the first four ribbons and then a little burp of laughter pops out of my mouth. I stop dead. There's no other sound. Nobody heard. I swallow the next giggle, but it's getting bad so instead of tying on the last four I just throw them on the foot of their beds and hurry out the door.

Now I'm in terror of doing the last two bunks. I can't trust myself not to burst out laughing. But I got to get a grip otherwise the whole thing is going to bomb.

These last two bunks are thirteen-year-olds, intermediates. The very last is the worst because that's where my adorable sister, Nina, is. If she wakes up I'm really absolutely lost.

Somehow I get through the first bunk and now all I have to do is El Creepo's bunk. I take a deep breath, then I take five more, and then three more, and then I know if I don't get started right this minute I'll be taking deep breaths till the dawn.

I count to my special lucky number. It's really mine alone because I'll bet there isn't anyone else in the whole world who uses forty-seven for her lucky number. But it goes too fast. I may change it to 147.

No problem getting into the bunk. I tie Nina's on first because I have to get that over with.

"Could I have a glass of water?" a voice whispers from the bed in the corner.

I freeze.

"Could I, huh?"

There's only one thing to do. I go into the bathroom and hunt around for a glass. It's even darker in the bathroom. I move my hands around on the shelf where they would probably keep the glasses. But I can't find any. This is horrendous. I don't know what to do.

Then I hear somebody getting out of bed. They're coming to use the bathroom. Please don't let it be Nina.

I open the door to the bathroom and stand behind it. The person goes into the toilet. She closes the door. I wait for her to finish and open the door. Then I grab it so she can't close it. She tries but I hold it. And my breath.

She tries twice, then I hear her padding back to bed.

I'm about to try to get out when I hear the voice again. "Big deal, can't you just get me a little glass of water?"

I start searching around again for a glass when I hear the slippers coming back to the bathroom. I jump behind the door again. This time the slippers stop at the sink. I hear the water. It seems like forever until she goes back to the other room.

"Thanks," a voice says, and then the slippers pad over to her own bed. There's a sound of springs as she climbs into bed and then quiet.

But she can't be sleeping. There's no way I can finish. All I care about now is getting out of here without being seen.

I wait a couple of minutes and then I start walking toward the door. There's no sound, and just as I reach the screen door, a very sleepy voice asks, "Where are you going?"

"To the bathroom," I say.

"Okay," she answers, and I slip out the front door fast.

Once outside I start running back to my bunk. It's beginning to get lighter out and we have to do our own bunks, otherwise they'll know in a minute who did it.

We're supposed to meet outside the bunk. Steffi's already there and Alexandra comes right behind me.

"How'd it go?" I ask them.

"Horrendous," Steffi says. "I couldn't do the last bunk because one of the kids was up with a flashlight when I got to the door."

Alexandra had trouble, too. One of the little kids woke up and had to go to the bathroom, so she took her. She was so groggy she didn't even notice the difference.

Except for a few people, maybe fifteen, we did everyone. Now all we have to do is get back in our own bunk, tie on some papers, and get back into bed.

This is the worst part.

We go into the bunk one at a time, very quietly. I go last. The minute I open the door my eyes shoot over to Dena Joyce. She's dead asleep on her side curled up like a baby. From this side it even looks like she's sucking her thumb. I tiptoe to my bed.

My eyes on D.J. all the time. Strangely enough from the other side she looks like she's sucking her thumb, too. What a thought. I tuck it in the back of my mind. It would make great ammunition.

Each one of us ties a paper onto the next bed just as planned. It's really going perfectly.

I love doing things like this. It's so exciting. I love an adventure because it's so dangerous. Can you imagine what would happen if Madame Katzoff or Dr. Davis found out?

I'm safely in bed when I hear D.J. move in her bed. I carefully turn around and there she is, thumb out of her mouth, eyes open, staring at me.

"I can't sleep," I say.

She doesn't say anything. Then, after a couple of seconds, she closes her eyes.

She probably wasn't even really awake. That's what I have to think or I'm finished. We're all finished.

I decide I'm simply not going to worry. So for the next hour I stay awake purposely forcing myself not to worry. It doesn't work.

But I must have finally fallen asleep because the next thing I know I hear voices, not close by, but outside the bunk.

Lots of voices, crowds. What's going on? And then I remember and jump up out of bed. Boy, do I remember.

I'm the first one up, but a minute later the twins get up. Right at the same time, too. And first thing they notice is the crepe paper and in two seconds they put the whole thing together.

"It's Color War!" Enid shouts. At least the twin in Enid's bed.

"Fantabulous!" Ellen says, jumping out of bed, and then everyone is up.

"Hey, wow!" Steffi says. Boy is she a lousy actress.

And so is Alexandra who overdoes it horrendously by jumping up and running around the bunk grabbing at the ties on everyone's bed.

Even though it's fake we still made the teams just the way we want them. Al, Steffi, and I on one team and the rest of them on the other.

I watch Dena Joyce closely. She doesn't seem so excited. In fact, she doesn't seem excited at all, but then again, she's always pretty cool.

"Fabulous," I join in the excitement, my eyes still peeled on D.J. She's looking funny. It's like she's observing us. "Who's on the green team?" I say, waving my crepe paper. "How about you, D.J.?"

"Right," she says, and without another word leaves the bunk.

She knows.

We're lost.

Al and Steffi both see what happened. She's going to rat on us. And there's no place to run.

The twins and Liza are still jumping around, but the three of us get very quiet.

"What do you think?" Al whispers to me.

"We just have to wait and see," I say.

"But what do you think will happen?"

I shrug my shoulders. We both look at Steffi.

"At best, the worst."

"Now I feel better," I say.

"You want the truth, don't you?"

Meanwhile, the twins and Liza have stopped jumping around. "What's up?" Liza asks.

The three of us trip all over each other to say, "Nothing." And then try to look very ordinary. If I do it as badly as they do, we're in big trouble.

"Something's fishy here," Twinny Somebody says, and her shadow shakes her head in agreement.

"Yeah," Steffi says, looking at Liza. "What's up?"

"Right." Al and I jump right into it, taking our cue. "Something's funny."

"I think so, too," the other twin says, and before you know it we're all standing around trying to find out what's happening. Except some of us know already, and nothing matters anyway since Dena Joyce *really* knows; and it's just a matter of time before they come with the Dobermans.

"Come on," Liza says. "Let's go find out what's up."

And the three of them go out leaving us unprotected. The minute they leave the bunk we fall into a hysterical laughing fit that's really sheer horrendous panic. And I mean fall, all over the beds, the floor; we can't get our balance.

We're going on like this for I don't know how long when suddenly Steffi stops. "Listen," she says, "listen how quiet it got."

It's true. Suddenly there's this weird silence. All that excited noise outside has stopped.

"What do you think?" Al is the first to ask, her eyes popping.

"I don't know," I say. "Look out the window."

"No, you look."

"No way," I say. "I got us into this. My job is finished. You both have to get us out."

"Do you think D.J. told or what?" Now Steffi is beginning to look as bad as Al, which is about what I feel in my stomach. "If she didn't it's only because she loves us so much. Come on, we're worrying too much. It was only a little joke; why would they take it so seriously?"

"Are you kidding?" Steffi suddenly gets very sensible. "Color War is heavy stuff."

Alexandra is shaking her head, agreeing, "Everybody really goes all out for it, so when dear old D.J. told them it was all a big trick, they probably went bonkers. Wait till you see, they're going to be furious."

"So what do you think is gong to happen to us?" I ask her.

"It's all according to who gets us first."

"Right," Steffi says. "If we can survive the kids, we'll probably just get a good talking to."

"That's not so bad."

". . . by Madame Katzoff?"

"It's horrendous!"

We all try to figure what she'll actually do. And we decide that no matter, she can't really do more than just fine us. I mean, they don't have capital punishment in summer camp. At least, it didn't say so in the brochure.

A little more conjecture and we end up in terror.

It's still eerie quiet out there and then slowly, far in the background, we begin to hear sounds. And they get louder, like the sound of a crowd of people in the distance. A big crowd, and crazy, like it's the French Revolution and we're King Louis the whatever.

"I'll choose you for who looks out the window," I say.

And while our whole castle is being stormed, we do one-potato, two-potato. Steffi loses.

She sort of creeps across the room and peeks out from between the broken shutters. "So?" I ask her when she gets there.

"Holy shit!"

Now Al and I race over to the window. Oh God, it's awful. What looks like hundreds of camper-type humans are spilling out from behind the last line of bunks and all converging on our bunk. And boy do they look angry. Remember unruly mobs from movies? That's the picture, and they're coming fast.

"Are the gargoyles with them?" Al asks.

"I don't see them," I say.

"Then we're okay."

Both Steffi and I look at Alexandra like she's off the wall.

"Are you kidding? Four million peasants in revolution and you say we're okay. What's going to happen when they get here and they're almost here right now."

"You'll explain," she says.

"Just say it was a little joke . . ." Steffi gets right in there.

"No, *you* say it was a little joke."

It's hard to believe those hordes of people are actually headed here. It's all ridiculous. After all, what are they going to do to us anyway?

And even though I know they really can't string us up

or anything like that, still the sight of all those angry kids out there is scary.

"Should we hide or what?" Steffi asks.

"Great idea," I say, and the three of us frantically start to search for hiding places. The crowd sounds are getting louder. God, it was only a little joke.

"This is dumb," I tell them. "Three people can't hide in this room. Forget it, they'll find us in a minute. Besides, it looks worse. It's like admitting guilt."

"What should we do?" Alexandra asks.

"Stay here and face it."

"Or what?" That's Steffi, of course.

"Or run."

"Let's go!"

And the three of us head for the door. We open it, look out, and slam it shut instantly. It's too late. Half the population of upper New York State is marching on us.

"Out the window!" I shout.

But the stupid broken shutters don't open. Nothing to do but face it bravely. That's probably what courage really is. No other choice.

We can hear the pounding and scuffling of the mob and then footsteps, a lot of them, coming up the steps onto the porch. Their mistake.

Then the shouts, "Watch it!" "Oh, shit!" and other exclamations as the boards crack and sink under their feet. We may have our own kind of moat.

Then the pounding starts.

"Open this door!" someone hollers.

"Shove the cubbie in front of the door!" Steffi says, and

the three of us slide Liza's cubbie against the door. Now the pounding gets even harder and more voices are shouting for us to open up.

"The other cubbie!" I call out to Steffi, but it's too late. They've already got the door partway open and nothing is going to hold it. We're done for. Incredible. This is nuts. Plain old campers don't break down doors. This is a nightmare.

Nothing left to do but give up. "Okay," I say, "since it was my idea, I'll go first."

"Right," says my best friend, "you go first."

All the time those nuts out there haven't stopped pounding and now the door is halfway off its hinges and splitting down the center.

We can see the enemy faces squeezing grotesquely into the partly opened door. Two more minutes and they'll be in. We've pasted ourselves against the wall as far back as the room will allow. I can't believe this all started from such a little joke.

"They're really nuts," I say to Steffi, and she just shakes her head. She can't believe it either.

"What are we going to do when they get in?" she asks me, and I can see she's scared. I am, too.

So is Alexandra.

A couple of more slams on that door and it's finished. Al looks like she's going to cry.

I'm beginning to feel that way too.

The shouts and the scuffling and the pounding and now a new sound even more terrifying. A high screeching noise, at first thin, someplace far in the background and then building in power, louder and louder and finally like a siren right in front of the bunk. The squeezed heads begin to pull out from the bulging door to turn in that direction, and the assault falls off a little. The door that was stretched open closes a bit, and the attackers let up. Huge relief.

We all run to the window but there's nothing to see. The crowds are turning in the direction of the Rec Hall. The siren is still blasting, but now we can hear another sound, like a drum and then a cymbal and then horns, and it's music. The siren is still blaring but dying out as the music comes closer. It's a marching band!

At first a few of the kids from the back of the crowd break away and start heading over toward the Rec Hall; then a few more leave. The first ones begin to pick up speed and then break into a run, then the others follow and more and more kids are turning and running in the direction of the music.

"What's happening?" Al says.

"Who cares?" I say. "We're saved."

And we are. In no time there isn't a soul left in front of the bunk. They're all running to the music.

"I know what it is," Steffi says, and at that moment it dawns on me, too, what's happening. "Color War, that's what."

"Only the real thing this time."

Alexandra is only now beginning to pull herself together. "Isn't that the weirdest, nuttiest thing? We get saved by the very thing that almost knocked us out."

"Don't count your chickens. We're not finished yet. Not

by a long shot," Steffi says, but she's smiling because the worst is definitely over.

"We made it. All they're going to do is fine us or something like that," I say.

But Al is still worried. "Yeah, but what's the something like that?"

"No big deal—I can practically guarantee everybody's going to be too busy with Color War to bother with our little nothing. You'll see, they're going to be laughing about it soon, right, Steffi?"

"She's right, Al. Maybe a fine, tops. Don't worry."

"Hey, you know what? It just hit me that Color War really *did* break. I'm dying to know what teams we're on. Let's see what's happening."

We have to practically drag Alexandra out of the bunk, but finally she comes with us and we all race down to the Rec Hall.

The whole camp is there. The band is marching around the lawn followed by some of the counselors dressed in clown costumes with huge helium balloons stretching up into the air anchored by long strings attached to their shoulders. They have baskets tucked under one arm and with the other hand they're tossing green and gray colored balls to the kids. Everybody is scrambling for them. Nobody pays any attention to us. One of the colored balls comes right at us and Al grabs it.

It's shiny, like a Christmas ball, and there's something inside. She twists it open and takes out the folded paper inside. It's the team lists.

"Quick," Steffi says. "Open it. I'm dying to know if Robbie's on my team, or what."

Me too, only I'm dying to know that he's not on mine. Boy, he better not be.

Alexandra goes first since she caught it.

"Green team, I'm on the green team! Here, Victoria, you find yours."

I get it in a second. "Green team, too. Great." I hand the list to Steffi. "Fingers crossed you're on our team too."

"Damn," she says.

"What?" I grab the list.

"Gray team. What about Robbie? You look."

I turn to the boys' part, and his name practically jumps off the page.

"I knew it," Steffi says. She's right, there he is, third from the top, on the green team.

"Sorry." And I really am, but it's no big deal. It's not like we're alone; there's at least a hundred and fifty kids on each team.

"That stinks. Everybody good is on the green team." Poor Steffi, she's really disappointed.

"Hey, it's going to be all right," I tell her. "You got D.J. on your team."

"Gross."

". . . and the twins."

"Both of 'em?"

"Both. And Dracula and the Wolfman and Erica from *All My Children*."

"That's enough," Al says, pulling me close to her. "No more consorting with the enemy."

"Up yours," Steffi snarls.

"Uh-uh, now where's your sense of sportsmanship?"

"Hey!" One of the little kids, maybe a sophomore, comes up from out of nowhere and yanks on my sleeve. "Aren't you one of the waitresses who did that thing?"

I shake my head no, but she's not one bit convinced.

"Oh, yes you are." And then she grabs her little friend and, pointing to me, says, "Isn't she that one from the dining room?"

"You mean The Spiller?"

"Yeah."

"Yeah." The other little one shakes her head. "That's her."

Nice. That's what I'm known as, "The Spiller." I wonder why.

"Boy," the first little one says, "are you in trouble. My counselor is really mad at you."

"So is mine," the other one says. "I'm going to tell her."

And the two of them run off and so do we. We head back to the safety of our bunk, fast. But not fast enough.

"Just a minute, you three." Without turning, we all know we're finished. It's all over. But when we do turn, we see there's still a little hope. It isn't Madame Katzoff or the Doctor. It's only Ginny Fowler, the head counselor. "I'd like to have a little conversation with the three of you. Meet me in my office in fifteen minutes."

And she goes off.

"She's okay," Steffi says. "She's been here for years. Everybody likes her."

Alexandra agrees. "A big talking to and a little fine. Don't worry, it's cool."

"We just got lucky," I say. "If it hadn't been for the real Color War we'd have been sunk. I'd love to get back at the Dena Joyce gross-out some way."

"It's tough, though," Al says. "It's like she's made of steel. No soft spots."

"Everybody has soft spots, you just got to find them."

"Dena Joyce?" Steffi shakes her head like there's no way.

But I have an idea. I don't say anything to them because it needs more investigation. But just maybe good old hard-as-nails isn't so breakproof. We'll see.

"Come on, let's get over to Ginny's," Steffi says. "The faster we get this over, the faster we'll be in the clear or what."

And, as Steffi would say, we all go off to meet our destiny or what.

Exactly as predicted, Ginny gave us the big talking to, but the fine wasn't so little. We each lost eleven dollars. Still it was better than being hanged, which would have been better than a chat with the gargoyles; so we got off easy. Steffi said one day we'd look back and think it was a fabulous adventure. I said I had some ideas, too, but she said if I even mentioned one they were going to turn me in.

That was yesterday. Today our mini–Color War scam is old news, because the real Color War is starting this morning. From the minute we get up this morning we're no longer just regular people; we're either green team or gray team. And we're all killers.

Everything for the team.

Starting with breakfast. Lineup at the flagpole is done by teams, with me on one side of the grass circle and Steffi and her teammates on the other. It's weird for us to be separated like this. At this moment Steffi has more in common with Dena Joyce than she does with me. Well, I guess maybe that's an exaggeration. Nobody could have more in common with D.J. unless except for maybe Godzilla.

I'm still not used to these early summer mornings in the country. They're really super-looking, fresh and green, and you get a wonderful feeling just standing there breathing in all that clean air; but it's really cold. I'm always shivering in these little uniforms. It's either the cold or dread of serving. I'm still terrible at waitressing. I can't seem to get the hang of it. But Anna, the counselor I'm always spilling on, is beginning to like me more. She says since she's been here she's lost four pounds. It's a form of eating anxiety. Truth is I haven't spilled anything on her in almost ten days. She's due.

One of the big problems is all the jumping up and down everyone does. Every two minutes the whole camp rises for some dumb thing or other; sometimes it's just to sing to someone or because they've won something or other. But they're always doing it, and I'm always just passing with my tray. Naturally, it creates a problem—either it's a shoulder under a tray or a head under a tray. Either one is good for a swing from the cleanup squad now known as Victoria's group.

This morning it all feels different. Exciting. I love the

competition. Instead of just walking to the Mess Hall we march down in our groups singing team songs. We've got a whole stack of them. Most of them are easy because they're set to old tunes everyone knows. Strangely enough, here we are marching across the lawn singing songs with a lot of rah-rah-rahs in them and not feeling like jerks. It's incredible, but I guess you get in the spirit, and besides, when everyone is doing something it doesn't seem so weird.

In the dining room we all still have our regular tables. But now everything counts. Even the way we serve.

We set up the tables and wait for the kids. You can hear them singing "Hats Off" as they march from their bunks. The change is really fabulous.

They come marching into the dining room and take their usual seats, but it's all completely different. It's like they're in the army they're so well-behaved. Even my tables are perfect.

I'd looked up Henry's name yesterday and he's on my team, and the terrible bully Steven is on the gray team. Unfortunately, they sit next to one another. Steven is still as mean as ever, and Henry still has his same problems, the big one in bed anyway. He's also not the most popular boy in the bunk. Steven sees to that. I wish I could think of some way to help Henry, but so far the only thing he can do is tough it out, which is very hard for him because he just isn't tough enough. And I don't think he ever will be, which is probably why I like him so much.

This morning he looks adorable—his shiny blond hair slicked straight back and his neatly ironed green uniform with the green knee socks. He's not the youngest boy in the bunk, but he is the littlest and the cutest. I wish he weren't so unhappy-looking. It's like he's on the brink of tears all the time. And much too quiet for a seven-year-old boy, except when we're alone, then he's practically a chatterbox and very smart, too.

Did I mention that along with Robbie being on my team, to make matters even more perfect, El Creepo is also on the green team? Well, she is. She's such a little snitch, she didn't even waste a second telling my parents about the Color War fiasco. They happened to call last night, and so naturally she tells them, and naturally they really didn't understand, and my mother said couldn't I stay out of trouble for just one minute and things like that. I didn't need that, really I didn't.

"Victoria, may I please have an egg instead of cereal this morning?" That comes from Fay Miller, normally a seven-year-old monster but this morning a saint. That's what Color War does; you see, if you don't stay in line you get demerits and that comes off the team score. They even count eating. They count everything, the way you dress, neatness in your bunk, the way you march, the way you sing; everything you do is all part of the competition. Normally Fay Miller would either scream when I brought her her cereal or if she was in a real mood, dump it on the floor. It's weird, I never heard her normal voice before today.

And that's the way it continues throughout breakfast. I'm almost perfect, too. I get everyone's orders right, I don't drop anything, I don't spill anything, and I don't bump into anybody—practically to the end.

Then, just as I'm serving the iced tea, Robbie walks by, smiles, and says hi. That's all it takes. I stop in midair, smile back, lose part of my stomach someplace around my knees, and most of the iced tea around my feet. I also lose a half a point for my team. Anna breathes a sigh of relief. Even though she's on the green team, too, at least she's still dry.

Why does even the sight of him make me so crazy? And it doesn't get any better. Something's happening to him, too, I know it. Like yesterday afternoon. It was really hot and a bunch of us were hanging out in the pool when some of the guys came over. Robbie was with them. I don't know where Steffi was, but she wasn't around.

As soon as I saw him I pretended to get very involved helping Alexandra with her diving; but I could practically feel his eyes on me. And every once in a while I would look up, and sure enough, there he was, looking at me. More like staring. Maybe he just thinks I'm an off-the-wall weirdo and he's fascinated, but that's not what I read. I don't want to say what I read, not even to myself.

On the way out, Steven manages to trip Henry. All his little cronies get a big kick out of that.

"You okay?" I bend down to help Henry.

He shakes his head yes, and then does a wonderful thing—he doesn't cry. That's an immense improvement for him. I think I have something to do with it, because he sees how terrible things are for me and how I'm holding up. It's like we're in it together.

"Don't you worry, we're going to get him one of these days, you'll see."

"I guess," he says, but I can tell he's not convinced; I'm not either. It looks like he doesn't stand a chance against someone like Steven, but maybe that's the way people always feel about a bully, which is probably what makes bullies so effective.

Not a great beginning for either of us today. Maybe it'll get better with the races. Both teams are meeting at the big playing field for a morning of all kinds of racing, from real track events to crazy things like potato sack races.

I'm a pretty fast runner so maybe I can make back the half point I lost for my team.

By the time we finish setting up for lunch and get to the field everyone else is already there and some of the races have started. In fact, the broad-jumping competition is over and the gray team picked up six points.

Since this is the first day, everyone is very excited and there's lot of shouting and cheering. Parts of Color War are really annoying, things like Steffi and I not being able even to stand together. We have to stick on opposite sides of the field with our teams. And it means that Robbie has to be over on my side. And there he is.

"Are you in any of the events?" he asks me.

I love you.

I don't say that, I only think it. In fact, I don't say anything; all I do is shrug my shoulders and make some dumb face that's supposed to mean, I don't know.

He looks at me with those totally awesome blue eyes that feel like they're seeing right through you. "Do you want to be my partner?" he asks.

Of course I want to be his partner—forever, but that's impossible.

"I can't," I say, and then regret it instantly. It tells too much, so I scramble to fix it. "I meant that you can't choose your partners, can you? At least I didn't think you could."

"You can for the potato sack race."

"Oh, I'd love to, but I have to leave early to set up for lunch. Gee, thank you anyway, it would have been really fun."

Shut up now, Victoria.

". . . I adore potato races, they're really great . . . just terrific." When I get nervous I just rattle on. "They're really fun." And on. "Too bad I don't have time, but I can't be late for setup . . . so I'll catch you later . . ."

"It's now."

"Huh?"

"The race is right now."

"Too soon. My foot will never be healed in time."

I can be very fast when I get desperate.

Of course he's confused. "Your foot? What's wrong with your foot?"

"Just a cut. Not too bad."

"Sorry. You seem to have a lot of trouble with your feet, don't you?" He's referring to my nonexistent sprained ankle of a couple of weeks ago. I don't know if he believed that one but he looks very suspicious this time. I can't believe he doesn't know what the problem is.

"Right," I say, and I feel a little annoyed with him for pushing me. It's the first time I've felt anything but dumb goofy lovesick about him. He must know we shouldn't be partners. Why is he doing this?

"You got to get in this race." From out of nowhere,

Steffi appears. "I don't care if it is my own team, I can't root for Dena Joyce and Wally Kramer or Claire and that geek Norman. C'mon, you two, are you going to get with it or what?"

"I'm ready, but Victoria's hurt her foot."

"Again?" Steffi says, and just from her look I know it'd better heal fast or we're back where we started two weeks ago with her thinking I don't like Robbie.

"Just a little cut," I tell her. "Nothing." Then to Robbie, "I hope I won't hold you back."

"What are you talking about? We'll kill 'em," he says. "Wait here, I'll be right back." And he runs over to grab a sack off the pile at the side of the finish line.

I give Steffi what has to be the goofiest smile ever sat on a face and say, "Terrific!"

"Is it really, or what?"

"Hey, yeah, you heard what Robbie said, we're gonna kill 'em."

"I didn't mean that. I don't know why I keep pushing you two together. My luck you'll probably end up liking each other so much you'll dump me."

My heart drops right to my feet.

"Oh, Steffi, that would never happen."

"Take it easy, Torrie, I was only kidding around. I know that would never happen. God, you're my best friend."

Then she laughs and I do, too, at least I try. I actually get a sick feeling just hearing her say that—it's too close for comfort.

I feel I should say something, but the only things that

160

come into my mind are too real and serious, so I settle for easy and meaningless. "Hey, gimme a break."

And then Robbie's back, so we both giggle kind of secretly and of course he wants to know what's so funny.

"You are," Steffi says lightly, poking Robbie in the ribs with her finger. Naturally he pretends to be mortally wounded and doubles over in what's supposed to be horrendous pain. Lover-type people always play those games together. I suppose it's cute to them, but it makes the other people feel dumb and left out.

Suddenly I'm in a funk. I'm tired of always being uncomfortable with people who are supposed to be my closest friends, at least Steffi is, yet all I ever feel is bad around them. Either I'm worried that what I feel for Robbie will show or I feel left out or . . . or I feel jealous. Might as well admit it because that's the truth.

"Hey, Torrie, are you dreaming or what?" Steffi says, pulling herself away from fun and games with Robbie. "Snap out of it, you've got a race to win."

"Let's try it," Robbie says, holding open the sack on the ground. "You get in first."

I step in. And Robbie steps in. And Steffi steps back to watch.

It's awful.

The feel of Robbie standing alongside me, his arm around my waist, mine around his, is almost unbearable. I must be bright red, my face is certainly burning enough. Nothing's happened yet, and I'm in a sweat. What a bad idea.

"Hang on tight," Robbie says, "and count with me so we can jump together." I don't trust myself to do anything more than nod. "Bend your knees and then throw yourself forward."

We both bend our knees into an almost crouch and then spring forward with all our might. He lands way ahead of me, dragging the sack and throwing me over so I have to grab onto him to keep from falling to the ground.

"Sorry," I say, and kind of crawl up him to get my legs untwisted from the burlap.

"It's my fault," he says. "I have to keep my jump down to your level. Let's try it again."

"See ya," Steffi calls out, as she heads over to the gray side of the field. "Good luck!"

One of the twins standing by hears her and shouts, "Hey, Klinger, which team are you on anyway?"

"Right. Gray all the way," she says, then calls out to us, "Break a leg."

That's theater talk for good luck, but if Steffi had any idea of the things that are going on in my head she would mean it for real.

Robbie and I are off. It's so hard and such a struggle to just keep up that I practically forget it's Robbie I'm clutching on to, which is funny since this is the closest I've ever been to him.

Then the rhythm gets easier and I begin to think of what I'm feeling. I'm holding his waist and I can feel his body under the T-shirt. It's very warm.

So am I, especially all up and down my arm, the one that's wrapped around him. And every time we jump up the whole side of my body touches his.

"Okay," he says all out of breath, "enough practice. Let's get over to the starting line."

"Okay." My first words since I got in the burlap sack. No danger of me charming him.

We get up into the lineup. There are eight other couples in the race, four gray team and four green. We each have to stand next to a couple from the opposing team. Naturally we get next to Dena Joyce, and does she give me a look when she sees who's in there with me.

"Where's Steffi?" she says, leaning over and looking down into our sack.

If I was red before, I just caught fire. Again, I'm speechless. It's all because of the guilt. But Robbie isn't thrown by her. He knows it's a nasty remark, he just doesn't know the history of it.

"What's your problem, D.J., you blind? Don't you see Steffi over there?" he says, pointing to where Steffi's standing. He says it jokingly, but there's an edge you can't miss. She doesn't. And she shuts up because Robbie's no pushover like I am.

He also doesn't seem to feel guilty, which makes me feel good—and a little bad. Maybe I was wrong about him. I guess I was reading something into his looks that really isn't there. It isn't anyplace but inside my head; and I guess that's where it better stay.

Ginny, the head counselor, announces the race, and we all inch up to the starting line.

"On your mark . . . get set . . . go!" And we're off, hopping, jumping, and falling all over each other, and getting up and jumping again. We're neck-and-neck with Dena Joyce and Wally, and going at top speed.

"Up, down, up, down, up, down," we keep saying in unison. "Up, down, up, down . . ."

We're so busy watching out for D.J. and Wally that we don't see Liza coming up on our other side until she knocks into us and we go flying into D.J. and all three sacks go hurtling one over another.

"Quick," Robbie says, grabbing me under the arms, "get up!"

We lose precious time, and now we're last; we have to catch up to the other five couples.

Up, down, up, down . . . we give it all we've got and we pick up speed. Two other couples bounce into one another and go down. Only three more ahead of us.

We're really in rhythm now. We're moving like one person. And fast!

One more couple down and we're third and gaining.

"C'mon," Robbie says, smiling down at me, "we can do it."

Oh God, I really want to do it . . . for you, Robbie. For you.

Up, down, up, down . . . we're second, right behind Claire and Norman. One good blast forward and we can pass them, but every time we try, they move over in front of us. It's too hard to swing over to the side; we'd lose too much time if we did.

"Straight ahead," Robbie says.

"Can't," I say. "We'll hit them."

"They'll move, you'll see . . ."

Down, up, down, up . . . we're nearly up to them and they're not moving. And then we take one huge leap and they lean out of the way and we shoot past them. We're in the lead! Twenty more feet . . . I can hear them breathing and grunting just inches behind us. I feel like they're going to fall right into us. I have no breath left; one more jump and I'm going to sink into the ground. I can hear the crowd cheering over my own huffing and puffing. I can't see them. I can't see anything except a blur of everything that keeps going up and down with me.

Just as we bend for the down part of our jump, Claire and Norman land on the bottom end of our sack, stopping us dead and then jerking us backwards onto them, which sends them flying down, tearing our sack as they go.

With one big wrench Robbie frees us, and wrapping the torn burlap around our waists we start off again.

The two other couples behind us are closing in, but we only have another couple of feet left to the finish line. Everybody is screaming. With one last enormous leap, we throw ourselves over the line, and then down we go and over and over, rolling on the ground. Hands are reaching out to help us, and then they're untangling us from the shreds of the bag.

"We won!" Everybody's shrieking and jumping up and down.

Including Robbie and me. We're hugging and leaping up and down and dancing around, and it's the most exciting thing.

"You won, you rats." It's Steffi and she's smiling, trying hard to be a good gray-team person but secretly delighted that we won, and probably especially happy because her friends are finally getting along together. It's what she wanted all along. And we are—the joy of winning and something else, something that's been stored up inside me for all these weeks, coming pouring out in the hugging and touching; something that I know I have to control but can't for the moment. Don't want to, but must.

I can't tell if Robbie is sharing any of my feelings. It's better if I don't know.

The rest of the races are a triumph for the gray team. With the exception of the twenty points we won in the potato race, all the winning points go to the enemy team. As of the first morning of Color War the green team is trailing by one hundred fifty points.

The afternoon doesn't help much. We pick up some points for volleyball and lose points on softball and basketball. By dinner we're very much behind. I serve in a complete daze. They're ordering fried potatoes and I'm dreaming potato sacks. All the progress I've made in the last weeks is down the drain.

At least my tables don't have to wait for their dessert; I bring it first—before the main course. I'm totally dense tonight. The kids love it, but Anna suggests I'd better get my act together or risk losing more points. I try, but every couple of minutes my mind drifts back to this afternoon and the excitement of Robbie. As long as I don't look at Steffi, I can enjoy my thoughts, but the moment I do see her, I feel horrendously guilty.

I'm the last one out of the dining room. No one waits because everyone has too much work to do. Steffi shoots off to work on some secret stuff for her team. I have to get over to the Rec Hall to help out with the scenery for the musical production. That's the big competition the last night of Color War. It's five hundred points so it can make all the difference.

There are about fifteen people, including Robbie, working on the sets when I get there. I make sure to say a nice hello and then move to the other side of the room. He makes no move to get near me. No repeats of this afternoon's mistakes.

We're doing flags of all nations mounted collage-style on a semicircular backdrop. We don't actually have any real flags except our own and a Canadian one, so the rest have to be made up from scraps of materials painted on canvas. Alexandra and I are working on the ribs, the pieces of wood that hold up the flags. It's just sticks of wood crisscrossed and nailed at the intersection. It's not the straightest looking semicircle if that's possible anyway, but it's good enough to give the illusion of something that wraps around.

"I'll sort out more nails," Al says, "and you go get a few more pieces of wood, okay?"

"Sure thing," I tell her, and head across the hall to ask Ginny where I can get more sticks.

"We've got a big pile of them in the little shed around the back," she says. "Robbie, can you stop for a minute and help Victoria get more wood out back? You know where it is, don't you?"

"Sure thing," Robbie says, getting up from his painting job. "Got a flashlight?"

"Use mine," Ned Weiner, his partner in painting, says, handing him a miner's-lamp-type light.

I follow Robbie out the back door.

If I planned this it wouldn't have worked. It's so silly that she picked Robbie of all people, that I have to smile, just a little one to myself. My luck, Robbie sees me smiling and probably figures this is what I want to happen. Under regular circumstances I would but not now. I swear I don't.

It's pitch-black around the back. The shed is about twenty feet behind the Rec Hall. When we get there Robbie holds the door open for me.

"Can you hold this for a second, please?" he says, handing me the light. "I just want to find the switch."

The room is jammed with all kinds of props for plays and tons of sports equipment. It's hard to tell where the wood would be. And Robbie's having trouble finding the switch.

"Do you think it's behind those screens?" I ask him.

"I found it already but it doesn't work."

"Should I go back and get another flashlight?"

"That's okay, you just shine it over here and I think I can get to the wood."

We start picking our way deeper into the clutter. Now if I really *had* planned this whole thing, then I would delicately trip over something and he would catch me in his arms.

But I didn't plan it, and besides I'm so solid on my Nikes it would take a wrecker's ball to knock me over.

"Watch your step," he says, turning to me. As he does, his foot slides off a pole on the floor and he loses his balance, grabs for the wall, misses, and comes crashing down. I catch him for a second and then his weight crumples me to the floor, with him on top. In my hands even the most romantic possibility turns into a mess.

"God, I'm sorry," he says. "Are you okay?"

"I think so, if you can just get up . . ."

"Right, sorry," he says, picking himself up and trying not to knock anything else over. "Here, watch your head." He bends over me, giving me his hand.

I take it. But as I'm getting up I accidentally tip over a screen, and as it falls he grabs me around the back and pulls me against him out of the way.

I'm in his arms. The wool of his sweater is soft against my cheek and the warmth of his body feels good against mine. He's holding me; my eyes are closed. I feel his face against the top of my head. Then I feel his lips. Somewhere in a far corner of my mind a tiny voice says don't do this, what about Steffi, but I don't move.

"Torrie." Steffi's name for me. Still I stay in his arms. With his free hand he gently tips my head back and his lips come down on mine. Softly, sweetly, his mouth slightly open against my lips that part to match his.

I feel an enormous rush of love for him, so strong I can't stop myself from putting my arms around him and holding him as tightly as he's holding me.

I know I've never felt like this before.

And then he says the very same words that are in my head, that he never felt like this before.

I don't want to think. I only want to feel how good it is. I slide my arms around his neck and his hands trace the sides of my body along the curve of my waist and down to the tops of my thighs. The kisses become harder and stronger—not just his, mine, too, and time falls out as we sink down to the floor, still holding each other.

We're side by side and we can't get close enough. His hand moves under my T-shirt along my bare skin; his fingers lightly touch my breasts. It makes me jump, not just from the coolness of his fingers, but because I know this is all so wrong.

"Please stop," I say, but I don't move his hands or pull away from him. I feel like I can't, and then his lips press even harder against mine and it's like I'm lost. How could I do this to Steffi? How could I? But I do it, and the harder he kisses me the more I want him to, and when his hands begin to wander down into the top of my shorts I don't stop him. I just keep kissing him as if that's going to drive everything bad away.

I can feel his erection hard against my thigh, and I know I should stop this—not just for Steffi, but for me too, before it gets out of control. I don't know him. He's not my boyfriend; he loves someone else. I've never been like this before with any other boy, not even if he loved me. I've wanted to be with Robbie since the first day I saw him. And even though I know all these things I still don't stop myself.

But he does. He pulls back away from me. "Torrie," he says, holding me by the shoulders and looking right at me. It's that same electricity that I can't ever get away from.

"This is what I felt when I first saw you. You did too, that day, I know it."

"I don't want to feel this way. It's wrong. It's horrendously terrible."

"There's nothing we can do about it. We can't change it."

"Yes, we can."

"How?"

"Like we've been doing. We do nothing, that's all. Just stay far away from each other."

"No way," he says and pulls me tightly to him. "No way." There's a terrible determination in the sound of his voice and the feel of his mouth pressing hard against mine. In a second we're hanging onto each other closer than before, closer than I've ever been to any other boy. I never let myself go the way I'm doing now. I want him to hold me in his arms. I don't want him to stop no matter what. That's what real love must feel like.

We're lying together on the floor, the length of our bodies touching, holding each other tightly, kissing; nobody's in control, not him and not me. I just keep letting things go, getting deeper and deeper and further away from myself. It's really heavy, I know it. I know how selfish it is, how I'm betraying my best friend, how heartbroken she'd be if she knew. I know all those things but the feel of Robbie, the possibility that he could be in love with me, just wipes everything else out.

I've never made love with anyone. I knew I wouldn't with Todd. I just didn't feel that way about him, but it's different with Robbie. It could happen with him, but I don't

172

want it to. I don't want to be in love with him. Right from the beginning I've been fighting it. But if he falls in love with me, I don't know if I'll be able to fight it anymore. I really want him like I've never wanted anyone before.

But the wrongness of it is terrible. And then that thought takes over.

"We're away too long," I say, twisting out of his arms and standing up.

"Wait," he says. "I want to talk to you."

"No." And while I'm still feeling determined I pick up a pile of the sticks and start off toward the Rec Hall.

"Wait a minute, Torrie." Robbie stops me outside the door. His hand is on my shoulder. I don't turn. I don't want to look at him, we're too close. I want to keep thinking straight.

But he turns me, and even in the semidark I can see enough of him to feel that intense pull again. "It can't be the same, ever. Not with Steffi. That would be a bigger lie," he says.

"She doesn't have to know. Nothing really happened anyway. Nothing that will ever happen again."

He holds my face in his hands and bends down to kiss me. I get an instant flash of that first day I saw him, when he got off the bus. That's what he did with Steffi. Just like that, bending down slightly to kiss her. I remember it. "Please, don't . . ." I slip out of his hands and start back to the door.

"Victoria, is that you?" A voice out of the dark. I get a horrible sick feeling. That's the worst voice I could ever hear.

I turn around to look in the direction it came from, but I don't see her.

"I thought so," she says, still not coming out of the dark. "See ya around."

"Who was that?" Robbie asks.

"Dena Joyce."

Everyone knows about Dena Joyce. Even Robbie. "Oh shit," he says, and I can see he's lost his cool. "What do you think she saw?"

"Enough." I feel like I could cry.

"It would take someone really rotten to go back to Steffi with this kind of thing."

"Don't worry, she is."

"Then I have to tell her first," Robbie says. "Now, before her birthday."

"What are you going to say?"

"I'll tell her the truth."

"About this—what happened tonight?"

"No, not yet. That can come later."

"What should I do about Dena Joyce?"

"Speak to her. Blame it on me. Say I came on to you, anything . . ."

"I'll try, but she's such a bitch I don't think it'll do any good."

"Try." Robbie pushes open the door. I hold it while he picks up a pile of the wood and carries it inside. He comes back for a second trip. I pick up an armload and together we bring in the rest of the sticks. A couple of people look up at us, but most everybody is too busy to bother. It's almost 8:30. We have been gone a long time.

174

The rest of the evening is unreal. I'm supposed to be crisscrossing sticks, but Alexandra ends up doing most of the work. I can barely think straight. She knows something's up but she can't ask. Strangely enough, it doesn't feel like anyone put two and two together about Robbie and me—no one but Dena Joyce.

I've got to talk to her tonight.

I know she's been over to the Juniors' bunks helping out with their songs, so I wait for her outside. I get lucky and she comes out alone.

"D.J.," I whisper to her.

"Didn't waste any time, did you?"

"I have to talk to you."

"Wonder what about." And just like that, she starts walking toward our bunk.

I catch up to her. "Look, it's really not what it looked like."

"Heavens no," she says in that really gross voice. "You were just giving him artificial respiration, right?" She's going to make me crawl.

But I'm ready to. I'll do anything, and she knows it.

"All I mean is that that was the first time and it just . . . it just happened."

"Sure thing."

It's hopeless. "Are you going to tell Steffi?" I come right out with it.

"Oh, I don't know. What do you think I should do? After all, she is a friend of mine and I think she should know about her so-called boyfriend."

"It would be horrible if she found out. I would do

anything so that she didn't have to know."

"Anything?" She practically licks her chops.

But I really will because besides losing Steffi's friendship, she would be so hurt it would be horrendous, so I say, "Yes, anything."

"I'll think about it," she says, and dances off into the bunk.

"Torrie." Two seconds later Steffi comes up behind me. "What's up with her?" she asks, motioning as the last of Dena Joyce goes into the bunk.

"Nothing."

"You look upset. Is something wrong or what?"

I tell her I have a headache. "I must be getting my period."

"Again?"

"Maybe not. It's probably just Color War getting to me."

Now it's really terrible, I mean with Steffi. I can hardly talk to her. All I can think about is what a rat I am, how I've betrayed her. And she trusts me so much.

"Come on, Torrie, get a grip. It's not that much of a big deal."

For a second I think she's reading my mind and it makes me jump, then I realize that she's talking about Color War.

"Was Robbie working on the scenery tonight?" Steffi asks me as we walk into the bunk. Of course, Dena Joyce hears and stops in the middle of pulling off her sweater. It makes a great picture with D.J. frozen into a listening position with her head inside her sweater.

"She never looked better," Steffi whispers to me, pointing to her.

I pretend to laugh, but I find myself a little scared to be caught laughing at D.J. Then it hits me what a bad position I'm going to be in with her—all the time. And boy, is she going to use it. I don't know if I can handle it. Like now, I pretend I have to rush to the bathroom. Am I going to spend the rest of the summer running off to the bathroom every time Steffi starts to speak to me?

I manage to avoid my best friend long enough to get undressed and get in bed, and then it's lights out and I can pretend to go right to sleep. Dena Joyce wishes me a special goodnight and happy dreams.

Just so happens I have a wonderful dream, all about Robbie and me dancing really close at someone's birthday party. It's fabulous until just as I'm waking up I realize whose birthday it was.

"I would love to borrow your leather jacket," D.J. coos, half in and half out of my dream. I try to squeeze myself back into the dream, but when she repeats herself it's very real and no more cooing, now it's the Wicked Witch of the East and I'm not messing with her.

"On the floor, the pile near the end of my bed."

"Thanks." She's back to cooing.

Later Steffi asks me how come I lent D.J. my good leather jacket. I have to set up something for the future because I think there's probably going to be a lot of borrowing from now on—in one direction anyway—so I'd better have a good reason to be nice to D.J.

"You know," I say, trying not to choke on such a big lie, "I think she's really changing."

"Yeah," Steffi says completely unconvinced. "Into what? A toad?"

"C'mon, Steffi . . ."

"Gag me with a spoon."

There's no way I can pull this off except by changing the subject quickly. "Did you have your strategy meeting last night?"

"Yeah, how about you?"

"Right after breakfast this morning. I got on the planning committee."

These strategy meetings are for a very important event of Color War. Each team tries to put their flag up on top of Mount Mohaph. The one who gets it up there first wins five hundred points. The only other thing worth that much is the musical the last night of Color War.

It's not a big-deal mountain, more like a little hill, but each team has kids standing guard from early morning until dark. You've got to get past about ten people to get up. It's really hard and usually it turns out to be a big chase; most years nobody gets there.

"You better come up with something great because we've really got a winner. Ken thought it up. He's really smart."

Oh God, if only she could like him. That would solve everything.

"And very nice . . ."

Maybe she can.

"And I can tell he likes me. *And* he lives in New York."

She sounds like she's playing with the possibility so I get right in there with the heavy guns.

"I think he's fabulous, really terrific."

She looks at me sort of surprised. "Do you?"

"Absolutely. He's super."

"Oh, Torrie, now I feel terrible. I didn't know you were interested. I would never go near anyone you were even the tiniest bit interested in . . ."

"Are you kidding? I'm not even the slightest bit . . . I mean, no way."

"But you said he's so fabulous."

"For you, not for me. He doesn't appeal to me at all."

"Me neither. Robbie's all I need . . . *ever!*"

"Excuse me, but I think I have to go to the bathroom."

"You *think* you have to go?"

What she says about Robbie being all she ever needs does it for me. Just like I predicted, this is going to be the summer of the bathroom.

"Excuse me, Steffi, I'll be right back," and I rush off.

It's simple to wait in the bathroom long enough for everyone to start leaving the bunk.

"Come on, Torrie," Steffi calls to me. "You want to be late or what?"

Now it's safe to come out.

"What do you think?" Dena Joyce asks me, modeling my jacket, practically drooling with pleasure.

Steffi makes a gag-me-with-a-spoon face, and Edna, the PA announcer, saves me with the waitress call, and we all start the stampede down to the flagpole.

The strategy meeting turns out to be very exciting, and

it takes my mind off Robbie and gives me some breathing space. Nance, Nina's friend, has a really great idea. She suggests that we get one of the little kids to dress up in somebody's sheepskin jacket, and then when it starts to get dark, sort of late twilight, pretend to be a furry little animal and crawl up the mountain real fast.

It sounds crazy, but if it's dark enough and the kid was really little he might be able to sneak up through the wooded part of the hill. We all decide it's worth a try. The only trouble is they need the right little kid. I say Henry, but everybody else thinks he's sort of a scared little kid. Everyone knows how Steven pushes him around.

"He's the perfect size," I try to convince them. "I think he's the littlest kid in the whole camp, and he's fast. I've seen him run." But they all have the same feeling about him, that he couldn't carry it off. They may be right, he does let everyone push him around a whole lot and he's always crying about something. Still, it would be so great for him to get a chance to prove himself. Boy, if he could do this, nobody would ever dare take advantage of him again, and he'd feel so good about himself and have such confidence that he might not even wet his bed anymore. Well, maybe.

We spend a lot of time trying to figure out who could do it, but Ronald Benter, the only kid who's really right for it, is too big. I keep pushing for Henry. Finally Alexandra says maybe we should give him a try.

"It's no big deal really," she says, "because chances are it's not going to work anyway."

Then everyone agrees it's such a long shot, so what, let Henry try.

"Let me handle it," I say. "We're good friends. I know I can get him to try. Besides, no one will notice if they see him with me."

They all say okay and one of the boy counselors offers to lend his jacket.

"You better hurry, Victoria," Al says. "We should really have him try to do it tonight. I hear the grays have a super good idea this time."

"I know where he is right now," I say. "See you later," and I hurry off toward the baseball field.

I come up from behind the bleachers and stop just out of sight. Naturally Henry is sitting on the bench. He's a terrible baseball player. No confidence.

"Henry," I call to him.

He looks around. I poke my head out and wave. He comes running over. He really is so cute—if only he would smile more.

I tell him about the plan and how it's a big secret and he's been chosen over everyone else. All he has to do is wear this fur wrapped around him and sneak up the hill with the flag tucked under his arm. It gets his usual reaction.

"I don't wanna."

"Come on, Henry. The worst that can happen is you get caught. So big deal, at least you tried. What do you say?"

"I don't wanna."

"Sure you do. It's your big chance to really win over Steven. You could be the hero of the whole camp. That'd be great, wouldn't it? Huh?"

He's got his head down and he's kicking the grass. He's in his pre-crying position; unless I can convince him fast I won't be able to get to him through the tears. And there's only one way to get to him. It's for his own good.

"Forget it, you're doing it." That's called the Steven-bully method. "I already signed you up." Combined with a little lie.

"But I don't wanna."

"It's too late. Your name is on it."

"Can't you erase it?"

"No way. Dr. Davis won't let me." I probably didn't need this last thing, but I'm in a big hurry.

"I'm scared."

I tell him not to worry, that I'll be with him and to wear dark pants and a dark T-shirt. "I'll pick you up right after dinner."

When I send him back into the game he's still on the verge of tears, but nobody notices because he's always that way.

I do my regular things for the rest of the day, but all the while I'm trying to work out some sort of plan for this evening. It gets dark at about 8:00 so it should be just perfect around 7:45.

Henry and I will go around to the wooded side at the base of the mountain, just far enough away so that they can see somebody's there, but not make out who we are. Now, in my head, this is the way I see it. Just before we get there, I wrap the sheepskin around Henry and then just pretend I'm out walking the dog. Forget it that nobody has dogs at camp, if somebody sees me with a dog they're going to figure that somebody *does* have a dog. Seeing is believing, right?

Okay, so I sort of play with my dog for a couple of minutes and then I pretend to throw a ball up the mountain. That's when Henry takes off. He runs up the side of the hill on all fours, supposedly after the ball. He's got the flag folded up under his arm. As soon as he gets out of sight he can get up and run the rest of the way regular. Once he gets to the top all he has to do is stick the flag into the ground at the side of the Mohaph flag. That's it; then he just walks down and I'll be waiting for him. Nobody will know anything until the morning.

It's in the bag. Even Henry can handle something as easy as this. Boy, if this works it's going to change his whole life. I just know it.

I work on the plan all the rest of the day, and by the time I'm ready to pick Henry up I've got it down pat. It's practically foolproof. Alexandra thinks so, too. At the last minute she lets the guards on our team in on it so they can help out if I need them.

I spend all the time it takes us to get from Henry's bunk to the mountain trying to build up his confidence, but he's nearly hopeless until I put him in the fur jacket. Then, magically, something happens; he turns into a puppy. In two seconds he's scurrying along through the tall grass at top speed with only his little furry back showing; he's not Henry any more, he's a real-live dog. The transformation is incredible. And when I throw the ball he chases after it and brings it back in his mouth. Nothing to do but pet him, so I do.

Meanwhile, one of the gray-team guards watching calls out to me, "That your dog?" And I know we have it made.

"Yeah," I call back.

"What's his name?" she wants to know.

I can't get involved because I have to get him going up the mountain in the next couple of minutes before it gets dark. The first name that comes to mind is Sport so that's what I tell her. Then she starts calling, "Here Sport, here Sport . . ."

Henry is so deep into his dog act that he starts performing for her. Oh no . . .

"Sport, come!" I shout to Henry, but he keeps making his little circles. If he screws this up I'll kill him.

"Sport, for God's sake, come over here right this minute. You dumb mutt!"

Lucky for us the guard turns out to be Christy Margolies, who is not known for her great brains, but even she has to see that this isn't one of your everyday run-of-the-mill poodle-type breeds.

And she does. "What kind of dog is that?"

I grab the first name that comes into my head, "A whiffle."

"Really weird," she says, stretching her neck to get a better look.

Now I'm getting nervous. Even Christy can't be fooled much longer. Just when I'm starting to lose faith in the whole dumb idea, Henry suddenly stops dead, walks over to the nearest tree and, brilliant kid that he is, lifts his leg.

"Yeah, a whiffle." She's one of those dummies who pretends to know everything. "I think my cousin had one."

"They're great with balls—watch," I say, and throw the ball as hard as I can up the hill. "Get it, boy! Go up there and get it! And bring it back for all of us."

And off he goes up the mountain with Christy cheering him on.

Later everyone had to admit it was brilliant. Henry was fantastic. He went up that mountain, planted the flag, and came down again—*with* the ball. I ran to meet him, scooped him up in my arms, gave him a giant kiss, and nobody ever knew what happened.

At least not that night.

The next morning the whole camp went crazy when they saw the green-team flag at the top of Mount Mohaph. We got five hundred points and Henry was the camp hero. It was fabulous. He was carried on people's shoulders all the way down to the Mess Hall. They made up a special song for him, and overnight he became a BMOC. And boy, did he love that.

Steven didn't stand a chance. He was finished. Kids were fighting to sit next to Henry, to stand next to him—everything. He was an instant star.

What a difference it made in that kid. All smiles. No more tears, and probably no more damp sheets either. He really had it made now. That was almost as good as the five hundred points that would go down in camp history.

I get a lot of credit, too. Only I'm too nervous to enjoy it. Especially with Robbie turning my stomach upside down, Steffi on my mind, and Dena Joyce on my back.

*As of tonight, the last night of Color War, the green team
is one hundred eighty-five points ahead.* We were trailing
badly until Henry's big flag coup. The last major event is
the musical, worth five hundred points. All we have to do
is pick up one hundred fifty-eight points and we win the
whole thing.

There are two parts to this event, the singing part and
the dance contest. I'm a pretty good dancer, but I decided
not to enter when someone suggested Robbie be my partner. That's all I needed, so I said I was too busy.

Robbie's in it, but he's dancing with Alexandra, who's
only all right. Steffi's very good, and she's dancing with
Ken. He may be good too, but I've never really seen him
do his stuff.

The musical part turns out to be really great. The sets
we made for our team are perfect. It looks like just what
it's supposed to be, lots of different flags. Even the ones
painted on canvas look real. I wasn't involved in any of
the music so it all comes as a surprise to me. I love it; even
the gray team has some good songs. It's a hard choice, but

the judges give us one-fifty and the gray team gets only one hundred. We're looking good.

Twenty couples enter the dance contest. The first and second place winners will share the two hundred fifty points.

Nina is dancing with one of the senior boys. She's not bad. Mostly it's because she's borrowed my style exactly. If she wasn't my sister I would think she was kind of cute. And if she wasn't dressed in my clothes from head to toe I'd like her even better.

Steffi and Ken are terrific. They're really a hot couple together. If only it were true. That would be the answer to all my problems. But it isn't. No matter how good it looks, it just isn't.

The judges are from the dance academy in town so they don't know anybody. Second place is chosen first. It's two seniors on the gray team. Now we *have* to win first place. But it's going to be tough because Steffie and Ken are really grooving, and they're fantastic.

I'm torn. I want my team to win and I've really worked hard, but Steffi is my best friend and it would be so great if at least she had this triumph. I guess it's really because I feel so guilty. I want her to win.

They start eliminating couples until they get down to five couples, including my own sister. She's getting terrific, but Steffi and Ken are really standouts. They've got some steps that I never saw before. They must have been practicing a lot lately. Here I go again, trying to make it something it's not just because it would be so neat. Instant problem solving, that's my line.

Now they're down to two couples, two green-team Superseniors who aren't bad, but not nearly as good as Steffi and Ken. The gray team's got it.

And they do! It's Steffi and Ken and they carry their team over the top. It's all over and the gray team wins!

The place goes crazy with all the screaming and jumping up and down. Through it all I manage to stay as far away from Robbie as possible. Every once in a while I catch him looking over at me, but I turn away fast. Last time I look he's with Steffi and then the band starts to play "Friends" and everybody joins hands and sings together. Color War is officially over.

I wish camp was.

Or at least Steffi's birthday. In three weeks, which also happens to be the last week of camp. She has great plans for her and Robbie. I'm even included in some of them. The whole thing is horrendous, and I dread it.

I may be wrong, but I think I sense something different in Steffi these last ten days since the end of Color War. She's quieter than she usually is, but it's mostly about Robbie that she's different. Normally she goes on and on about him, but lately she hasn't been talking about him much. Maybe it's just me. I run every time his name comes up. In fact, that's what happened just now. We were sitting around after lunch doing our nails; Alexandra, one of the twins, Steffi and me, when D.J. comes wiggling into the bunk.

"Victoria," says Miss Obnoxious of the World, "I think I'm coming down with a sore throat. Could you do me a huge favor?"

"I guess so." I try to make it as inconspicuous as possible, but everybody hears. They all turn around in unison and look at me as if I just went bonkers.

"If you could just do my mail delivery today and tomorrow it would really help sooo much . . ." I don't know why she bothers, but she smiles. Maybe she's just happy. I would be, too, if I didn't have to do that lousy job.

It's too much for Steffi. "Why don't you just take an aspirin? A sore throat is no big deal, you know."

"I didn't ask you." No smiles now. "I asked Victoria. Do you want to do it or not?" she says to me.

"It's okay, I don't mind." Then I turn to Steffi. "Really, I don't mind."

Steffi shrugs her shoulders like, do what you want, and I get so nervous I spill the whole bottle of glorious pink all over my shorts.

"So." D.J. gives Steffi one of her triumphant looks. "What's up with Mr. Wonderful lately?"

My cue to exit—and fast. "I'll get an early start on that mail." And I'm off and out the door dripping Glorious Pink all the way.

I'm halfway to the main office before I feel safe enough to slow down to a walk. I have to do something about D.J. She's blackmailing me like in a movie. It's incredible that she knows how to do it so well. I never could—I'd feel too bad for the person. Besides, I'd be embarrassed to do something as dinky as that, but she takes to it so naturally.

"Torrie!"

I know without turning it has to be Robbie, the only other person who calls me by that name. I've been successfully avoiding him for over a week now.

I stop, take a deep breath, and turn. "Hi."

He catches up to me. "I have to talk to you."

"I'm just hurrying now. I have to sort mail and then I've got, uh, I don't know . . ." Suddenly I can't think, but then I decide I'm going to go with the truth. "Actually, I don't want to. It was all a terrible mistake and I'm sorry it happened."

I watch those earnest blue eyes start to squint up in pain while I say these things to him.

"I know what you mean," he says, "that's why I've got to tell her."

"About us?"

"No, not if you don't want me to, but I do have to talk to her about what's happened between her and me."

"What are you going to say?"

"I don't know. I'll just tell her the truth."

"That you don't love her anymore?"

"I'm not sure if I ever did. I think she thought she loved me, but we were apart a long time. Things change in a year . . ."

"You mean it was different when you saw her again?"

"Yeah, it was, even before you. Sure, I still liked her, but not like before."

It's not much, but it does make me feel a little better knowing it wasn't only me that ruined it. I tell him that, and he says I shouldn't feel guilty. He's the one who let Steffi down.

This is the first time I've ever had any kind of conversation with Robbie where I wasn't running off, or so uncomfortable because of how I felt about him that I couldn't think straight.

He is a nice guy and I can see he feels really bad about Steffi. I'm not sure how he feels about me. I know he's attracted to me, but I don't know if it's any more than that. Maybe that's all it is with me, too.

"I think maybe you jumped to conclusions about me," he says.

"How do you mean?"

"Maybe made too much of a simple attraction because you weren't supposed to feel it."

"I've never been so miserable since I met you."

"Me, too," he says. "That week when you were on dock duty . . ."

"Wasn't that horrendous?"

"The worst." His face gets very intense with that special look that grabs you so you can't turn away. "There wasn't a minute in that whole week when I didn't know you were there. No matter what I was doing, you were in my head. I kept thinking I got to cool this. It's crazy." Then his eyes let me go and he shakes off the seriousness with a smile. "One more rainy day and I'd have gone off the deep end."

"You're lucky," I say, and I'm just as happy *not* to have to tell him what I felt, "one more day like that and I'd have pushed you off myself."

He's back to serious. "Why didn't you say something?"

"I don't know. I guess I was still fighting it. Why didn't you?"

"I wanted to, but I kept thinking what if I misread you. What if you *really* didn't like me?"

"I know what you mean. I was thinking the same thing."

"I could just picture it. There I was, your best friend's boyfriend making a pass at you. You'd have probably spit in my eye."

"My problem is I probably wouldn't have."

"What about now?"

"Now is something else. I don't know what's up anymore. Anywhere I turn looks bad." And I tell him how terrible it's been; how it bugs me all the time, every time I see him, and how it's getting so bad that it's even beginning to sneak into my times alone with Steffi. "I have to do something. Make a choice one way or the other."

"I know which way it's going to be."

"Tell me."

"It's not going to be me."

As soon as he says it, I know he's right. And so does he.

"No matter what you decide," he says, "there's one thing I have to do. I have to tell Steffi before her birthday."

"That's horrible. She's been planning this for weeks. Can't it wait until after?"

"No, it can't. I feel like I'm lying to her and that's the worst of all. At least I owe her the truth."

Watching Robbie struggle with all this and knowing how horrible it's making him feel and what it's done to me makes me see something I didn't see before. I try to tell him.

"Somehow talking to you about all this takes some of the scare out of it. I know I like you, I can't pretend I don't, but it's really no good."

Then I tell him how it's not Steffi over him but it's the important things inside that you've got to listen to or everything comes out terrible. When you say honor and loyalty and stuff like that everybody thinks you're talking baloney, but they're wrong. It really matters. And getting something you want by betraying someone important to you just doesn't work. I know Robbie really is a nice guy and he feels awful about Steffi, too, and he knows I'm right.

"Did you talk to Dena Joyce yet?" he asks.

"Not yet. But I've got to do something quick. It's terrible."

And I tell him what she's doing to me and he's furious. Still, there's nothing he can do. "Turn the tables on her," he says.

"Are you kidding? She's invincible. She's like made of steel."

"Everybody's got a soft spot, you just have to find it."

"That's exactly what I used to think, but you don't know Dena Joyce," I tell him. "Which reminds me, I better get to her mail delivery or I'm done for."

"Am I going to see you again?" he asks when I get up to leave.

"You can hardly avoid me in this place."

"I don't mean that way."

I look at him, this gorgeous person I've spent the last six weeks agonizing about, and I think that all I have to do is say the right word and I've got him.

"No," I say. "I'm sorry but I just can't." That's really the right word.

"I'm sorry, too," he says. "What about letters?"

"What about them?"

"Will you answer if I write?"

"I don't think so," I say, much too fast for any real thinking.

"I'll take my chances," he says, and one look at him and I think I'm starting all over again.

But I'm not going to. "Gotta run," I say, and without looking back, walk—very fast—toward the main office.

I'm practically crying. I feel terrible, but I think I did do the right thing. Damn! It's very hard to do right things.

My head is jammed with so many problems that voluntary
mail sorting takes me half the afternoon. By the time I'm
ready to deliver the letters, everyone else is finished.

I go through my rounds in a daze. The only thing that
wakes me up is Henry's bunk. It's incredible to see what's
happened since the flag business of Color War. The new
Henry never stops smiling. Unreal.

"Hi, Victoria!" he says, giving me a running leap hug
outside his bunk. He's got two little bunkmates in tow. I
get hugs from them too. From here on in anything Henry
does must be right. And best of all, Steven got his. He's
absolutely out. Henry is the new big shot. I love it.

Except there's no end to the dog story. I must have told
it four hundred times already and they still bug me to tell
it again. Actually, I love to because it's so great to see how
Henry glows.

They drag me over to the porch steps, and with Henry
propped on my lap, I do the whole thing for the four
hundred and first time.

"Come on, kids," I say, trying to pick them off me, "I got to move it. I'm really late."

"How did Henry know to lift his leg?" Peter, one of his little converts, wants to know.

Of course, I've answered this same question before, still they ask like it's brand-new. "Because he was doing dog thinking. Show them, Henry."

And in a flash he turns back into Sport, and with the other two following every step, he runs off from tree to tree. It's really a gas.

The JC is watching. He doesn't look like he thinks it's so adorable.

"Don't you think it's terrific what happened to Henry?" I ask him.

"Sure, for Henry it's great."

"Then what's wrong?"

"Look at them," he says, pointing to the three kids racing around on all fours. "It's like running a kennel. And the constant barking . . ."

"Still, it's worth it. He's completely cured."

"Are you kidding? It's worse than before."

"You mean he still wets his bed?"

"Every night. But now because he's the big trend-setter, the other two do, too. It's like sleeping in a rain forest. Thanks a million."

I shrug my shoulders, tell him I'm sorry, and beat it out of there. I still think it's totally awesome, and absolutely the best thing to come out of an otherwise horrendous summer.

And speaking of horrendous summers, I have to do something about Dena Joyce. I have an idea. It's really desperate and maybe it's dumb and certainly it's mean, but nobody deserves it more. I got it from what Robbie said about finding a soft spot. I think I found one. I'm not sure I can pull it off, but I've got to try. Otherwise she's going to tell Steffi everything, I just know it.

And I really don't want Steffi to know about what happened with Robbie. It's terrible enough that he's going to break off with her. If she knew about me it would be the total end of our friendship forever. I just couldn't face that. I really couldn't.

Two seconds after I come into the bunk she's on me, Dena Joyce, that is.

"Honey"—that's the name she uses when she's about to chop off my head—"I think I'll keep your leather jacket for another day, okay?"

"No."

"Huh?"

"I said no."

"Are you sure?" I love to watch her face. She's shocked, but she's cagey; she smells a rat.

"Absolutely."

For a second she looks very surprised, then she begins to freeze up. "Are you sure? That could be a big mistake, you know." Now she's solid ice. I'm almost sorry I started, she's really scary, but I have to do it.

"Positive," I say.

"Okay." Ice smiles, throws my jacket on the floor, and turns to Liza, who's on her way out the door. "Did you see Steffi?"

"Yes," Liza says. "She had to meet Robbie about an hour ago. She should be back soon."

"Thank you," D.J. says, looking directly at me. "I'll wait here for her."

"Sure thing," Liza says, and goes out the door leaving me alone with Miss Dracula.

"Want to change your mind?" She gives me one last chance.

Now I've rehearsed this scene in my mind a million times since I thought it up this afternoon. In my head, this is the way it goes. It's the same so far, except now I tell her that I'm not about to change my mind, and, in fact, I was thinking I might like to wear her silk shirt—for the rest of the summer. Of course, she looks at me like I'm nuts, but she's getting a little worried. She knows I've got something up my sleeve, but she doesn't know what. And I play it out. I let her try to guess. I sort of tease her very subtly. I'm really in control and she's beginning to feel it. She begins to get nervous because I'm so cool. Finally, she knuckles under. She can just feel my power and I never have to tell her what I know. I really defeat Dena Joyce, probably the first time in history. That's the way it goes in my head. In real life it's a little different.

She's standing there with her hands on her perfect hips and an annoyed look smeared across her face. It's horrendous to confront Dena Joyce. All my plans fall into the toilet and all I can say is something on about Henry's level. "If you tell Steffi about me and Robbie, I'll tell the whole world you suck your thumb."

"Right," she says without missing a beat, and, cool as can be, picks my jacket up off the floor, carefully places it on the end of my bed, flashes me a Dr. Davis–type smile, turns and leaves the bunk. Totally awesome. Her losing is like anyone else's winning. It's so brilliant that I find myself wanting to run after her and apologize—*with* my jacket. I would make America's worst blackmailer.

But I did stop her. I stopped Dena Joyce. Probably the bravest most fantastic thing I ever did. Only trouble is nobody will ever know.

The minute D.J. walks out the door, Steffi comes in. She looks sick. Her face is dead-white except for her eyes— they're all red and swollen. Of course she's been crying.

"Steffi . . ." I don't know what to say. I have to pretend I don't know. God, I hate these lies between us.

She sits down on the edge of my bed and begins to sob. It's horrible. Heartbreaking.

"What happened?" I have to ask.

Between tears she tells me everything I already know about Robbie and the breakup, and besides feeling awful I have to pretend to be shocked. I ask her as few questions as possible and just try to comfort her. She knows I feel terrible because I'm crying, too.

"I don't know what happened," she says. "I knew something was wrong, but I didn't expect this."

I just keep listening.

She goes on about how terrible she feels and I can see she's really crushed. Then she gets kind of angry. "You know what I really think, Torrie?"

Suddenly I get a very bad feeling that I do know what she really thinks.

". . . I think it's someone else."

"No," I say. Then I say no again because I just don't know what else to say.

But she's convinced. "It's true, Torrie, it's definitely someone else, and I think I know who. What about you?"

My stomach falls about eighteen floors. "No, no, no," I say.

"You don't know who it is or what?"

I can't even get the little word "no" out of my mouth. All I can do is shake my head—and hope it falls off.

"It's Alexandra," she announces.

"Who?"

"What do you mean who? Alexandra, my supposed friend right here in my own bunk. What do you think of that?"

"It's not true," I say, and it comes out somewhere between it's not true, meaning it can't be, and it's not true, meaning it isn't.

She takes it to mean it can't be and says that it is. "It has to be her."

"It isn't."

But she pays no attention to me. "Boy," she goes on, "she really has to be a shit; I mean it. Sure, we're not best friends, but we've been pretty close all this summer. I can't believe she would do such a thing."

"She didn't."

Now she hears me. "Well, who else could it be? He hates D.J. He practically never said a word to Liza, and he can't tell the twins apart either. There's nobody else possible."

Here it is. I've got my choice. D.J. would never tell so I don't have to be worried about that. Certainly Robbie wouldn't. I'm safe there. Nobody's on my case. We don't even have a week left to camp, and then Alexandra's off to Connecticut and we'll probably never see her again. Nobody ever has to know the truth. Steffi and I can still be best friends.

I can't do it.

I'll probably regret it forever, but I have to tell her. No matter what. So I do. "You forgot someone," I say.

She's really confused. "Who?"

"Me."

I never saw anyone's face crash down like Steffi's does when that sinks in. First she looks at me like I'm kidding, then like I'm crazy, and then, worst of all, like I'm some kind of monster—which, of course, I am.

After that there's nothing more to say. I can't even explain anything because she stops crying, gets right up and walks out.

She hasn't said a word to me since. This has to be the most horrendous, horrible, gross summer of my life.

That all happened ten terrible days ago. Even though Steffi didn't say anything to anyone, everyone seems to know. I guess it wasn't hard to figure out, what with Robbie and Steffi breaking up and her not talking to me. Gossip is flying around like crazy.

One thing for sure, D. J. hasn't said a word. She's making wide circles around me. I really got her number. Too bad I can't think of any way to use it. Truth is I don't want to. At least I can say I'm not a blackmailer. I feel like I'm everything else horrible. I don't blame Steffi in the slightest.

I really miss her.

But she doesn't seem to miss me at all. She spends most of her time hanging out with Alexandra *and* Ken Irving.

I know the Ken Irving thing has got to be pure rebound. Steffi's not about to jump into another intense relationship so quickly after the Robbie disaster; still, they do look great together. He looks at her the way I used to look at Robbie. Which I don't anymore. Not to say I'm cured, because I'm not by a long shot. I'm still horrendously miserable, but it's different now. Before I used to think about Robbie all the time, now I can't get Steffi out of my mind.

I know all about wanting what you can't have and all that, and maybe it was a little like that with Robbie, but not with Steffi. She was my best friend for ten years and now she hates me: that really hurts. Every time I think about it I get sick to my stomach. It's gross.

And the thought of Robbie liking me doesn't help all that much, even if he is going to write to me, which is not absolutely certain anyway. Besides, if he really does write, then I have the awful problem of whether or not to answer him.

It's like I never learn. Here I am agonizing about Steffi and starting all over again about Robbie. It's cuckoo time, that's what, and I'm head cuckoo.

On top of all that I keep wondering how Steffi really feels inside. She's certainly putting on a good show. She's even gotten friendly with one of the twins. Suddenly she can tell them apart. I think she's pretending, but whatever, she seems to be recovering pretty good. Better than me. Yesterday I even saw her talking to Robbie.

I spoke to him one last time yesterday. He's still pushing for us to get together. No way. I still think Robbie Wagner is terrific, really, but maybe he's not as special as Steffi made him up to be. Maybe nobody can be that perfect. I'll bet she doesn't think he's all that great anymore, either.

It's not that Robbie and I don't speak, it's just that I keep out of his way. No big deal about it, it's just easier that way.

Ending camp is a pretty emotional time. Even for me, and I can't wait to leave. Madame Katzoff and Dr. Davis get up to give their farewell speeches (actually Dr. Davis just nods) but Madame Katzoff wishes everyone a good winter and to come back next year. The whole camp sings the "Hats Off" song and there's lots of cheering and applauding. I'm beginning to think they weren't so bad after all until they start reading off our accumulated fines for the season.

Out of the $260 salary I walk away with a big $180. A real bomb summer.

Except for one nice thing—Henry. I go over to say goodbye to him. He's just doing so great I really feel proud about how he's changed. That's the best thing that happened this whole summer.

There's lots of hugging and kissing and promises to visit in the winter. He really is a special little boy.

I watch him walk off toward the buses, one arm around his new friend's shoulder and the other dragging his plastic bag with the wet sheets. He's a changed kid—well, almost.

I go back to my bunk and nobody's there. I guess everybody's off saying goodbyes. That's okay, I've been keeping mostly to myself lately anyway. I had so much time I answered all my mail for the whole summer, only it's so late I might as well take them home with me.

I'm just packing the last of my stuff when Nina comes in. Just what I need.

"What do you want?" I ask her. Might as well get it over with as fast as possible.

"Nothing," she says, and sits down at the end of my bed.

"So?" I try again.

But she just shrugs her shoulders.

"So what are you doing here?"

No answer.

"Okay, what do you want to borrow?"

"Nothing."

"Come on, Nina, what's up? I got things to do."

She turns bright pink and gets up off the bed. "I just wanted to say that . . ." She starts inching her way toward the door, ". . . that . . ."

"That what?"

"That I really love you and I'm glad you're my sister." All in one breath and she's out the door and gone.

Weird.

But I guess sort of nice. At least somebody still loves me, even if it is only my sister.

When I go over it in my head later, it makes me feel pretty good. I never think of Nina as a real person, but I guess maybe she's starting to be one.

Real nice.

Everyone knew I was in a funk, but she's the only one who actually tried to help me. It took guts, too, because I'm not always so terrific to her. Especially when I'm not feeling fantastic anyway. I guess there may be something to say for family. Maybe it's not so bad to have her around—sometimes.

Just when I'm packing the last of my things I find my blue vest. I've never been so crazy about it, and I hardly ever wear it, so instead of me lugging it home, I drop it off at Nina's bunk. She's not there so I dump it on her bed and leave.

Walking back I get a warm good feeling inside when I think of how surprised, more like stunned, she'll be when he sees it. Warm and good enough to make me smile for the first time in a lot of days.

18

Now's the time I'm really dreading—getting on the bus. I feel like nobody's going to want to sit next to me. I don't blame them. It's like I'm a little girl again and I'm the last one chosen for some team thing. It's almost tears time.

That is sort of what happens. I get on the bus, go all the way to the back, and find a seat near the window. People start getting on and taking seats. Everybody seems to have someone to sit with. Everybody but me.

I look out the window and see Steffi, late as usual, walking to the bus with Ken. They're talking and laughing, having a great time. I feel awful. Not because they're happy, but because I feel so sad about Steffi. We've been best friends for so many years, we shared so many secrets, so much of everything, and now it's over. It's one of the saddest days of my life.

I watch her climbing on the bus. I keep my head down. I can't even look up to see her coming down the aisle. I can't because I don't want her to see me crying.

I'm studying the toes on my Nikes and wishing the bus would get started. It's really gross to be sixteen and be catching tears with your tongue, but if I wipe them with my hands everyone will know what's happening.

"You want company or what?"

Or what. The two best words in the English language. I don't even have to look up to know that fabulous voice.

"Absolutely." I nod my head and give Steffi one very wet smile. Then I wipe my face with the back of my sleeve, which is really gross, but things like that don't count with best friends.

Meet Glenwood High's fabulous four, the

SENIORS

Kit, Elaine, Alex, and Lori are very best friends. On the brink of graduation and adulthood, these popular seniors are discovering themselves, planning for the future, and falling in love. **Eileen Goudge $2.25 each**

___	#1	TOO MUCH, TOO SOON	98974-4-13
___	#2	SMART ENOUGH TO KNOW	98168-9-19
___	#3	WINNER ALL THE WAY	99480-2-18
___	*4	AFRAID TO LOVE	90092-1-17
___	#5	BEFORE IT'S TOO LATE	90542-7-21
___	#6	TOO HOT TO HANDLE	98812-8-27
___	#7	HANDS OFF, HE'S MINE	93359-3-27
___	#8	FORBIDDEN KISSES	92674-2-19
___	#9	A TOUCH OF GINGER	98816-0-15
___	#10	PRESENTING SUPERHUNK	97172-1-23
___	#11	BAD GIRL	90467-6-22
___	#12	DON'T SAY GOODBYE	92108-2-31
___	#13	KISS AND MAKE UP	94514-3-19

YOUNG LoVe®

IS A VERY SPECIAL FEELING

- _____ **AND BOTH WERE YOUNG,** Madeleine L'Engle $2.95 90229-0-21
- _____ **CAMILLA,** Madeleine L'Engle $2.95 91171-0-35
- _____ **CLOSE ENOUGH TO TOUCH,** Richard Peck $2.50 91282-2-31
- _____ **I SAW HIM FIRST,** Marjorie Weinman Sharmat $2.25 94009-5-03
- _____ **IT'S NO CRUSH, I'M IN LOVE,** June Foley $2.50 94212-8-14
- _____ **LOVE BY ANY OTHER NAME,** June Foley $2.50 94738-3-19
- _____ **MY FIRST LOVE AND OTHER DISASTERS,** Francine Pascal $2.25 95447-9-59
- _____ **RONNIE AND ROSEY,** Judie Angell $2.50 97491-7-50
- _____ **SECRET SELVES,** Judie Angell $2.50 97716-9-67
- _____ **STARRING PETER AND LEIGH,** Susan Beth Pfeffer $2.25 98200-6-43
- _____ **UP IN SETH'S ROOM,** Norma Fox Mazer, $2.50 99190-0-68

Norma Fox Mazer

*explores the limitless
need for love
we all face.*

___Dear Bill, Remember Me?	91749-2-20	$2.50
___A Figure of Speech	94374-4-42	$2.25
___Saturday, the Twelfth of October	99592-2-47	$2.95
___Someone to Love	98062-3-16	$2.95
___Summer Girls, Love Boys	98375-4-26	$2.50
___Up in Seth's Room	99190-0-68	$2.50